The Road of a Thousand Tigers

Robert Craven

The Road of a Thousand Tigers

Copyright © Robert Craven 2018

All rights reserved. No part of this book may be reproduced, stored in a retrieval system or transmitted in any form by any means without prior written permission of the publisher or author, except by a reviewer who may quote brief passages in a review to be printed in a newspaper, magazine or journal.

The right of Robert Craven to be identified as the author of this work has been asserted by him/her in accordance with the Copyright Designs and Patents Act 1988.

The novel is a work of fiction. The names and characters are the product of the author's imagination and resemblance to actual persons, living or dead, is entirely coincidental. Objections to the content of this book should be directed towards the author and owner of the intellectual property rights as registered with their local government.

Books

The Eva series:

Get Lenin.

Zinnman.

A Finger of Night.

Hollow Point.

Steampunk:

The Mandarin Cipher

The Road of a Thousand Tigers

For

Sam Blake

> *No man can step into the same river twice,*
> *for the second it is not the same river*
> *and he is not the same man.'*

Heraclitus.

ONE

Cairo 1956.

A mosquito hovered, its drone nothing but a whisper. Sebastian Holt pincered his fingers toward the stealthy little insect. He crushed it between thumb and forefinger, rubbing its remains between them. Through the open window, the first calls of the muezzin's prayers drifted out over the slums and buildings of the capital. Holt threw himself from the bug-ridden bed and walked to the shower. It sprayed water in tepid bursts allowing a brief sensation of coolness on the skin. After the shower Holt stropped his razor along the shabby strap. He shaved in cold water. The face staring back through the cracked mirror looked older than twenty-three years; but that was because sleep had been a fitful few hours. Holt dried himself with the threadbare towel giving his thick mane of hair a flick of the comb. He shrugged on a smart twill jacket and checked the breech of his Browning 9mm. He took his travel kit, spare ammunition clips and placed them into a small duffel bag. Glancing one more time around the room, he shut the door.

The corridor was dimly lit, the one flickering lightbulb indicated some level of electrical power was pulsing through the city. The rickety elevator groaned on its journey to reception. The hotel foyer was deserted. Holt turned a sharp left to a room where a slice of light flickered from under the door. He opened it without knocking.

"You shouldn't have shaved, Chaiwallah," said McGowan.

No names, no uniforms; just nicknames – McGowan was 'Paddy', the leader. Holt because of his black hair and colonial gait went by 'Chaiwallah'.

"There's little by way of breakfast. A few re-heated stale flat breads, compensated, I must say, by strong coffee," said McGowan.

A long-handled coffee pot stood sentinel beside a bread basket and a stack of delicate china cups. McGowan had a city-grid map of Cairo and photographs spread out on the dining table. He was lean and in his late thirties. He produced a silver hip flask and poured its contents into two cups,

"The one lesson I learned in the desert, Chaiwallah, was that like Rommel's Afrika Korps, both are equally unforgiving. Drink up, its good scotch; the booze will keep your circulation tickin' over in the midday heat,"

He tapped the map with a long, pointed pencil,

"Now that Nasser has thrown his lot in with the Russians, her Majesty's government is keen to remove some very sensitive material without drawing too much attention. We know now that the consular safe house is known to Egyptian intelligence, which means the Russians aren't far behind."

McGowan tapped the map with the pencil. Holt sipped the coffee.

"Rooke's 2nd Para are holding this area here. There'll be a Westland landing at 11:00 hours,"

"That doesn't give us much time," said Holt.

"Or anyone else," said McGowan, "We'll be an escort service for a young lady and a strongbox. A sealed strongbox with official secrets that must never see the light of day on this, or any other continent," said McGowan, his rolling Irish cadences hanging in the air, "Any questions?" he asked.

Holt shook his head. He tried to visualise the route.

"Best not keep a lady waiting," said McGowan.

He folded and tossed the map to Holt,

"Think you can get there, Chaiwallah?"

Holt smiled. They left the hotel.

Holt felt the sheer naked power of the Mercedes 120w pulsing through the steering wheel. McGowan reclined on the plush back seat. Holt pulled up to an old style French colonial house. It was a broad belle epoch mansion with ornate Rocco-style pillars fronted by a large smooth lawn. The sun cast a long streak of sunlight across the doorway. Holt and McGowan got out, went to the boot and took out two Thompson machine guns. They walked up the gravel drive. The Thompsons hung from their sides. They looked up and down the street.

"Turned out nice again Chaiwallah," said McGowan.

"Just like New Delhi,"

McGowan stopped on the pathway.

"Yes, just like New Delhi," he said.

Holt wished he'd kept the engine running. He checked his Rolex Tudor Gold, a gift from his mother; it was 6.30am.

The door opened.

The girl standing there was breath-taking. A thick blonde plait fell from under a broad brimmed summer hat. Her capri pants and ballet pumps made her look like a blonde Audrey Hepburn, but taller.

"It's inside," she said.

Holt and McGowan went inside the house and found a huge metal-plated strongbox. They wrestled the box into the boot of the car. The girl slipped into the back seat, tossed her hat aside. Her legs were long and shapely.

The boot clunked shut and Holt jumped in and started the engine. Holt handed his machine gun to McGowan who sat beside the girl. McGowan slid the Thompsons across the floor.

A gloved hand appeared at Holt's shoulder. He shook the hand but stared ahead.

"They call me Sam," said Samantha,

"They call me, Chaiwallah," said Holt.

"I recognise you," she said.

Holt waited.

"Cambridge, a year ago," said Samantha, "You gave a talk on hand guns,"

Holt stared at the glasses in the rear-view mirror

"I hate guns," she said.

Her voice was light and cultured, but he thought she could deliver a hearty shout.

The Mercedes left the elegant suburbs and arrived at a dense, bustling free-for-all of an ancient metropolis coming to life. Carts, horses and donkeys competed with buses, cars, bicycles and motor-bikes for any available space. There was no left or right-hand lane, only a gap which was dashed at by all at a merciless speed. Holt weaved the Mercedes through the melee, keeping a steady speed. He tapped the rear mirror.

"Two Packards have been on my tail for the past three minutes," he said.

In his rear-view mirror two identical tan-coloured Packard Cavaliers parted the morning rush hour traffic like knives.

"That's the bloody Ismalia, lose them, Chaiwallah and I'll pay for the drinks," said McGowan. Holt pulled his Browning pistol from its shoulder holster and dropped it between his legs on the driver seat. He tossed the pistol's two magazines from his leather jacket on the passenger seat.

"Brandy and champagne," said Holt.

The needle on the speedometer slid to the right. Holt careered through three junctions at high speed. Pedestrians were dodging, and horns were blaring when the back window shattered. The next bullet hit the rear-view mirror. Holt pressed his foot on the brake, locked the steering wheel to the left and wrenched the handbrake. Like a capsizing motor boat, the Mercedes spun one hundred and eighty degrees. Holt floored the accelerator.

"Plus, a Havana cigar," he added.

He hit the first Packard. The Ismalia lost control of their vehicle, it pitched upwards, hurling the four occupants onto the street. The second one slewed. It disappeared behind street stalls and café awnings. Holt worked the gears into reverse. Somehow, the rush-hour commuters weaved around the chaos as Holt straightened the Mercedes up.

One down, one to go, he thought

McGowan and Sam clung onto whatever came to hand.

The remaining Packard was more dogged. It appeared out of nowhere, almost colliding into the back of the Mercedes.

"They're going to a lot of trouble over that box, Miss Barnes," said McGowan.

He cleared the remaining shards of glass and the car was filled with the sound of him returning fire.

"What's in it?" shouted Holt over the gunfire and screeching brakes,

"Ciphers, codes and transmission data from our Tel Aviv station to London." said Barnes.

"Suggest you lie yourself on the floor then, Miss Barnes," shouted Holt.

"No, I will bloody well not!" she shouted back.

Holt swerved to avoid a donkey and cart. The animal reared, tossing the contents and the driver onto the street. Wrestled free from its harness, it kicked and jumped in blind panic blocking the Packard's progress.

"I thought we weren't supposed to be drawing attention?" said Barnes.

A bullet ricocheted around the car, coming to rest in the panel above her head.

McGowan put a hand on Barnes' thigh, smiled and said, "We'll be alright,"

Barnes pushed the hand away from her capri pants and smiled.

"They've found us again," said Holt, "Could we switch with another car?"

"That box is too heavy, Chaiwallah," said McGowan, "We're out of time. The helicopter will hold for ten minutes tops,"

The machIne gun began firing again.

Holt accelerated and swung around the road trying to make the Mercedes a tricky target. The two cars, the pursued and pursuer, cleared the city limits and a long stretch of road appeared. Holt could see the Packard was accelerating alongside.

Samantha Barnes pressed herself deeper into the corner of the back seat. McGowan was sweating as he picked up the second Thompson.

"Miss Barnes, can you take the wheel?" shouted Holt.

"I thought you chaps had done this before?" she shouted.

"No choice, I'm afraid," said Holt.

"Still know how to show a girl a good time then?" she said.

Samantha Barnes clambered into the front of the car and Holt pushed across to the passenger seat. The Packard was alongside. One *Ismalia* agent, all mirror sunglasses and beige suit took aim at Samantha's profile. Holt propped the Browning pistol across his arm and fired point blank. The mirrored sunglasses disintegrated, and the Packard veered hard away off onto the scrub.

The rendezvous bounced and shimmered on the horizon. It was a flat piece of land with a sandbag perimeter. Two parachutes lay unfurled in the sand making an X framed by a few desolate palm trees. Holt reloaded as McGowan spotted the Packard swinging back in from behind and angling toward Barnes' side. Another burst from his Thomson was met by loud bangs and cracks. McGowan slumped across the back-seat. The front of his shirt was doused in blood. His eyes were wide open as if caught in a camera flash, his lower jaw just bloodied meat.

The Thompson lay smoking across his lap.

Holt glanced over at Barnes. Her sunglasses revealed nothing. She stamped on the accelerator. The needle on the Mercedes surged past 120kph.

"You really don't remember me, Chaiwallah?" shouted Barnes.

"I'm a little preoccupied, Miss Barnes," replied Holt.

"We had dinner together in a pub. Near Queens Street."

"The Mason's Arms?"

"Yes, Chaiwallah Holt."

"I remember it well,"

"No, you bloody-well don't, Holt."

From the back-passenger window, the beige Packard's nose appeared. A burst of machine gun fire riddled the Mercedes' roof. The remaining side windows shattered and thuds of bullets hitting the side panels shook the Mercedes' chassis.

Holt emptied another magazine in return fire.

He fumbled for the Browning's last magazine. He cursed under his breath as a few rounds spilled onto the floor.

He fired a few probing bullets into the bonnet of the bucking, bouncing Packard.

They had little effect.

"Take this, Holt." said Barnes.

Barnes reached to her neck and tugged, handing him a fine silver chain and crucifix,

"My family live in Cambridge, Chaiwallah,"

"There's the helicopter," said Holt.

A huge Westland Whirlwind clattered overhead toward the sand-bagged clearing. It hovered over the rendezvous like a fat bug. The Packard was now alongside. Holt fired across Barnes' face until the last magazine clip ran empty.

"I'm out," he said.

Samantha Barnes tugged the steering wheel colliding with the Packard. The *Ismalia* driver forcing her back onto the road. She set her jaw tight and put everything into pushing back. Holt leaned in and added his weight to the wheel. A bullet from the Packard shattered the windscreen.

Holt smashed the rest of the glass away and he and Barnes leant closer in for a better view.

They cleared a rise and the landing zone came closer. Holt squinted at the silhouettes trotting into position.

They were setting up a machine gun nest.

"Brake! Now! Brake for Christ's sake!" he shouted.

Holt pulled up the handbrake as Barnes stamped her two feet on the brake pad. The Mercedes stopped hard. The Packard flashed ahead and drove straight into concentrated withering machine gun fire. It idled into a small gulley. Two more bursts from the nest and the car ignited.

Reaching back, Holt checked McGowan's pulse - he was dead. Holt sprinted around and opened the driver's door. It was when he unbuckled Samantha he saw her wound. Her blouse was soaked with blood

"Damn, Holt, damn..."

Two soldiers dashed past them and opened the boot.

She slumped into his arms. He could smell her perfume as he unfastened her seatbelt. Easing her out, Holt dashed towards the helicopter with her cradled in his arms. The helicopter began to increase its rotations.

A soldier barking orders stopped and strode towards them.

"Colonel Rooke. Best get aboard, son,"

Rooke's face was dusted by the desert, like the rest of his men. He motioned for two squaddies to assist them.

"McGowan?" asked Holt.

"Have to leave him, son," said Rooke, "did enough to get you here. A good man,"

The troopers were mounting the Westland and a medic had Samantha Barnes stretched out on the floor of the helicopter. Her complexion was as white as her shirt.

"Sorry, she's gone," said the medic.

In less than an hour, they were high over the Red Sea. Colonel Rooke looked at his watch and nodded. Two troopers man-handled the strongbox to the open doorway. The ocean swirled far below. They brought over Samantha Barnes and secured her legs to the box with strong ropes.

"Wait, no!" said Holt

"She knew the risks, this is the deal," said Rooke.

If he was upset, it didn't show in his hooded eyelids and sagging crow's feet.

The strong box was nudged over, then pitched over the side. It fell towards to ocean. Samantha Barnes' long blonde plait fluttered in the cold Arabian skies.

Holt opened his bloodied hand. Her silver cross shone like a tear-drop. He closed his eyes and rested his head against the helicopters vibrating airframe. The soldiers' heads were all bowed in silent prayer.

"Mission accomplished, son," said Rooke.

"I hope it was worth it," replied Holt.

"Where will we drop you off?"

"Somewhere where I can get a bloody good drink. You can start with Cambridge," replied Holt.

"We can get you started," said Rooke.

He removed his helmet revealing a creased forehead and a smooth-shaved pate.

A small ripple below marked Samantha Barnes' resting place,

"She never had a chance," said Holt.

"None of us have," said Rooke.

The Westland clattered toward the aircraft carrier that appeared on the horizon below. The ocean closed over the weighted strong-box and it plummeted into the dark depths with Samantha Barnes in tow.

TWO

Prague - 1958

If Hugo Ostrovsky was worried, it didn't show, but his guts were churning. A car meant official business, a Russian car meant official Russian business. The rain hammered down in sheets leaving small explosions of water along the church steps of the headquarters of the STB – The Czech spy service, known by their Moscow overlords as *'The dangerous little brothers'.* In the grimy twilight, the nearby Vltava River broiled and churned in the unseasonal downpour. A sudden squall shook and battered Ostrovsky's umbrella and he needed his two hands to steady it. His wire frame glasses dripped rivulets of water down his weak chin with its trimmed red goatee. His socks were a freezing swamp in his soviet factory-made shoes. Ostrovsky mentally ticked off the numerous reasons why Feiks Povlovich Sukhachen would be arriving from Moscow, none of which was satisfactory. Why had Sukhachen wanted him? Why not a higher-ranking officer? Had he offended his Russian 'Uncles' with some counter-revolutionary action? Was he destined for a Siberian death camp? If he dwelt any longer on these matters, his bowels would have loosened. He regretted having such a heavy lunch. Ostrovsky inhaled a deep rain-sodden breath as the bulky Zil pulled up. He trudged down the steps and opened the rear doors,

"Honour the work, comrade!" he shouted over the gale.

The man who emerged from the car and crouched under the umbrella, Director Sukhachen, waved a dismissive leather glove,

"Honour, yes, we honour the work, comrade," he growled.

"Welcome, comrade Sukhachen,"

Sukhachen was tall and lean and well dressed in a dark suit, the new breed of KGB officer that had emerged from the shadows over the years. Groomed and mannered by the English defector Maclean, they were no longer bumbling, blood-thirsty peasants. They were a more urbane kind of creature; lupine but just as unfeeling and lethal. Director Sukhachen trotted up the church steps and into the cloistered shelter. He appraised the stained-glass windows and the ancient paintings of saints with the air of a connoisseur.

As Ostrovsky wrangled the umbrella shut and jabbed it into the holder in the coat stand, Sukhachen handed his herringbone coat to an STB guard.

"Allow me to introduce Natalia Kvashnin," said Sukhachen.

Ostrovsky hadn't considered for a moment that the KGB director would have had a companion.

"I'm sorry, comrade, director, it was dark... I didn't see..., your driver didn't say anything, comrade," he started.

Again, the imperious wave,

"No need, no need – please, Comrade Natalia!" motioned Sukhachen.

Ostrovsky gave his glasses a cursory wipe on his damp shirt sleeve and peeled them back on to his head. He blinked twice at the figure in the doorway.

Natalia Kvashin was tall, almost too tall for a woman. Over six feet in height, she was dressed in misshapen olive combat fatigues. A clump of wiry fair hair was pinned back with a forage cap tilted and pinned at an extreme angle. A military kit bag was slung over her shoulder as she glided in. She was somewhere between a prima ballerina of the Bolshoi and a wrestler, but the splice was somehow incomplete. The almond-shaped eyes beneath intelligent brows were a deep amber; a sliver of her Georgian heritage, with tiny pupils that took everything in with a glance. Her lack of make-up, poise and manner suggested her age could have been anywhere between thirty and sixty. She didn't smile, or nod, she saluted.

"Comrades," she said.

If a python could speak it would have sounded like Natalia Kvashnin, thought Ostrovsky.

"Comrade Kvashnin was one of the legendary 2nd Moscow Women's Battalion of Death," intoned Sukhachen, "She fought with distinction against the Kaiser's forces in the great war of the trenches, before her remarkable talents were spotted by Chief Dzerhinsky and put to more effective use for the Bolshevik revolution. She has just transferred from Kolyma."

Natalia puffed her chest out, her gaze unwavering at some spot in her middle distance.

"Now, Ostrovsky, time is of the essence? Let us now honour the work." said Sukhachen.

"I've arranged refreshments, director,"

"Splendid, Ostrovsky. Splendid," said Sukhachen.

In a bishop's ante-room with a long oak desk, Ostrovsky ushered them to high backed chairs and closed the door behind them. A portrait of Lenin addressing seamstresses, peasants and sailors loomed from a far wall.

"Comrade Director, from the continent of Africa to the highest echelons of Western democracy…" started Ostrovsky

"Yes, yes, yes, Ostrovsky, Moscow is aware of the sterling work the STB does," interrupted Sukhachen. He reached for the silver service on the desk and stirred the thick cream into his coffee, "I represent Department 5 of the KGB; the cultivation of assets in France. Therefore, myself and comrade Kvashnin are here to talk to you. You have such an asset under cultivation in Paris, yes?"

Sukhachen's 'Yes?' sounded like a direct threat.

"Yes, comrade director, the asset has filtered several pieces of disinformation to the editors of numerous publications in the country," swallowed Ostrovsky.

Natalia sipped her coffee black, her hands were thick, her fingers unadorned, fleshy and muscular. Her amber eyes never once left Ostrovsky.

"Please provide me with the status of your department's disinformation?" said Sukhachen.

Ostrovsky dialled an internal number with a shaking hand from the aged desk phone. Within moments a knock at the door was followed by a furtive officer already sweating into the room,

"The delay was unacceptable!" barked Ostrovsky.

The officer bowed and apologised, his comb-over falling loose over his ear. He placed a file in the middle of the table and stepped backwards still bowing.

Sukhachen shrugged off his jacket and rising, placed it on the back of the chair. His waistcoat and pants were exquisitely cut, not clattered out on a soviet industrial sewing machine. His tie was silk, tie clasp and cuff-links gold. Ostrovsky became aware of how damp his threadbare socks were.

"This is excellent, Ostrovsky. For our VESTNIK colleagues along the Auguste-Blanqui Boulevard?" said Sukachen.

"Among other news outlets, comrade,"

Sukhachen spread out the doctored images; French government politicians frolicking with underage girls and boys. Shadowy pay-offs in cafes and underground car-parks. Grainy pictures from brothels of leather and studs.

"We have some of the best photographic labs in the Soviet Union, Comrade director," said Ostrovsky.

Reams of typewritten stories and by-lines were ready for the teletype and telegraph exchanges of Paris. Sukhachen flipped through them pausing at any salacious paragraph.

"Indeed, indeed – I'll get to the point. Your asset has gone missing."

"Missing?" said Ostrovsky.

"Missing. Gone. Missing. Your asset, our enemies call *'Cochise'* has disappeared," said Sukhachen.

"That can't be?"

"Oh really? Why not Ostrovsky? Why is your asset *not* missing?"

"I spoke to him,"

"When?"

"Yesterday,"

"When yesterday?"

"Morning. Early. He radioed in at the correct time, on the correct bandwidth, correct code. Everything was correct,"

"Correct?"

"Yes, very correct, comrade director,"

Ostrovsky had moved past worrying about his damp socks. His shirt was stuck to his body from sweat. Natalia could smell it. Her nostrils twitched as she placed her cup down.

"I'm afraid everything is very far from correct, little brother, Ostrovsky. Very far," said Sukhachen.

He walked towards Ostrovsky. Natalia, lithe and agile was already at his side.

"Moscow has lost contact with him and we think he's trying to run. Plausible as he's American. Run to where? We don't know – back to America, Britain, or thrown himself at the mercy of the local branch of the SDECE? Who knows?"

Natalia delivered a blow to Ostrovsky's solar plexus that knocked the wind out of him. Clutching the air like a drowning man, he sprawled to the floor. She followed through with a vicious kick to the gut. Ostrovsky fought on three fronts; to keep his breath coming in, stay conscious and not release his bowels. All were on the verge of capitulation.

"Moscow wants this situation addressed. You've met this asset, face-to-face, yes?" said Sukhachen.

Yes' now sounded like a death knell.

"Yes, comrade director, I have," gasped Ostrovsy. He tried to ball himself up but Natalia's well-timed heel to the groin stopped that. He yelled out despite himself.

It reverberated around the cathedral's high vaulted ceiling and walls.

"Well then, well then, comrade Ostrovsky, my little brother, Ostrovsky, you see my dilemma? You see Moscow's dilemma? Our mutual dilemma? If your asset turns, all my department's work is for naught. All of Russia's work is for naught. Understand?"

Natalia reached down and with surprising strength gripped Ostrovsky's wet collar and hoisted him up. With slow deliberation, her wiry arms locked around his neck and with measured pulses began to constrict her muscles.

They were like a vice.

"You must think of humanity, Ostrovsky, humanity past, present and future as one great body; a body that requires surgery," said Sukhachen.

Natalia's constrictions continued.

"Now, Ostrovsky, you cannot perform surgery without severing membranes, destroying tissue and spilling blood," continued Sukachen, "We need to constantly perform surgery on humanity, bring it all under one brotherhood of revolution,"

As he gasped for air, Ostrovsky's bowels gave up the fight. His bladder surrendered too. Sukhachen, stepped back in disgust and from an inner pocket of his waistcoat, pulled a silk handkerchief to his nose,

"You will travel to Paris, find your asset. Ensure they tell you everything they know, everyone they have spoken to. Eliminate. Return here. Comrade Kvashnin will accompany you and ensure you follow through."

It was the last thing Ostrovsky heard before he blacked out.

The smell didn't bother Natalia, she had smelled much, much worse in the basement torture chambers of the Lubyanka prison and the far-flung gulags of the USSR.

Sukhachen walked to the door and opened it.

"Mr Ostrovsky has had an accident, he requires assistance,"

He skirted Ostrovsky's bodily fluids and seating himself farthest away from Ostrovsky's prone form, finished his cup of coffee.

"Vasha Zdorve, Ostrovsky," he said.

THREE

London

Caxton Petrie wasn't accustomed to being summoned. The government car in the street below had an arm hanging out of the window, flicking a cigarette. With the sleeve rolled up, the arm had taken on the distinct colour of boiled lobster.

Petrie closed the shutters to his office. He preferred the dark. Stepping over to the long red leather clad desk, with its two phones; one black and one red, he turned off the desk lamp. He straightened the leather blotter and stowed away his magnifiers and pens in the drawers beneath.

"Ready when you are, Archer," he said into the desk phone.

He digested the communique in his hand. Stamped ULTRA, it came directly from the PM and the FO. He creased it into four and inserted it into his inside pocket.

Petrie's secretary, Elizabeth Archer knocked twice and entered. She was dressed in stylish sensibility for the unseasonal spring. Her hairspray melded with the miasma of old tweed, beeswax and pipe tobacco. Once she had been a barrister, now Petrie entrusted her with the leather-bound intelligence files. He deflected her concerned glance with a wry smile,

"The man in reception is beginning to become impatient," she said.

"I'm sure he is," said Petrie, "a little white rabbit from the mandarins of Whitehall. Does the rabbit have a name?"

"His name is Harrowby," said Archer.

She spun on her elegant heel in a slow-burn fury. Petrie took down his Macintosh and donned it in a smooth movement. It was a coat of superior manufacture; the cold nights at sea on convoy duty had given his blood a permanent tinge of ice, requiring an extra layer of clothing no matter what the weather. This tincture of ice, he believed, allowed his mind and his heart to authorise actions without remorse in the name of the greater good. He pulled on an old-fashioned Bollman hat.

"Good hunting, sir, bring me back a pelt?" said Archer.

She flattened down the mackintosh's collar in brisk efficient movements.

"I'm thinking more of a scalp, Archer," said Petrie.

The man from the ministry, Harrowby, waiting beyond her organised desk, fidgeted in his seat. He rose as Petrie walked past him. Harrowby then found himself trotting behind and wrestling his briefcase into a more manageable angle. His ill-fitting suit and pasty face seemed to compound his general disarray.

The ministry car with the lobster-armed driver swept along Pall Mall, Hyde Park and turned towards Whitehall. Petrie worked a pipe cleaner through its stem before tamping a snatch of tobacco from a pocket pouch into his pipe and with a lighter puffed to ignite it. Harrowby clasped and unclasped his hands, he watched Petrie out of the corner of his eye. The car pulled into the kerb. Harrowby got out first. He held the passenger door then trotted like a faithful hound behind Petrie. A well-dressed receptionist stood up and marched around his desk. He was regimental right down to the waxed tips of his moustache,

"May I take your coat, sir?" he asked.

"No, you may bloody-well not," replied Petrie.

"Very good sir, take the lift to the top floor, sir,"

The elevator lurched up to the top floor and wheezed its doors open. Petrie strode down the corridor. Dust motes hung in the air as the sunlight pierced the dirty windows. Frosted glass panels to his left portrayed misshapen denizens flitting through the rooms like odd-looking eels in a tank. The burly man, no doubt armed, standing at the last door opened it in a measured fashion,

"Good afternoon, sir," he said.

Petrie was ushered into a room so compact that his desk would have had to be dismantled without any guarantee it could be reassembled to fit the confined space.

"I take it this isn't a social call, then?" said Petrie.

"Take a seat, Petrie, it won't be long," replied the Permanent Under-secretary. His name was Laidlaw. A direct conduit to the Secretary of State for Foreign Affairs.

Laidlaw gestured to the man sitting behind the modest sized desk,

"This is minister-without-portfolio, Dewar."

Dewar, like Laidlaw was well dressed, clad in privilege and power. He had a faint dusting of dandruff around the collar.

"Fancy a Dimpled Haig?" asked Laidlaw.

He produced three tumblers from the desk drawer and poured three hefty fingers,

"I'll get to the point, Petrie. The PM is utterly furious, utterly - at the Suez shambles. As a result, we have lost the trust of our cousins across the Atlantic and have made some very unsavoury enemies in the Middle East."

Dewar, from a black case at his side produced a manila file,

"Em, because two of our very best have skipped over the iron curtain, the Prime Minister suggests a net be cast for a more refined type of agent. One who can sniff out the new breed of KGB. The Russians and their SMERSH section will now have their operatives embedded in the west, groomed by Maclean to blend in. We'd like you to look at recruiting a higher-ranking individual – a good background, preferably aristocracy, but having combat experience?" he said.

His accent had traces of Afrikaans, his skin mottled by a lifetime in the sun.

"What may I ask, are you suggesting, sir?" said Petrie.

Laidlaw quaffed a generous measure and then urged Petrie with the empty tumbler to sit.

"I, we, the minister and I, need to understand your department?" said Laidlaw.

Laidlaw had the virile middle-age demeanour of horses and hounds and unfortunate debutantes who fell into his nasty little sphere. He produced a packet of Dunhills and lit one up. His hand had a faint shake as he tapped the ash onto the dusty floor.

"I'm allowed a certain amount of latitude and I keep three officers on active service – I have three on assignment now. One of them hasn't reported in yet," said Petrie.

"Um, how many agents have you in total?" asked Dewar.

"They are intelligence officers, and as to their number - that's classified, I'm afraid," said Petrie.

"Any women agents?" asked Dewar.

"Classified,"

"The Russians and Israelis are well ahead of us in that regard," said Laidlaw.

"Again, classified," replied Petrie.

"We believe there are nine in total and since Burgess and Maclean, the average life span of one of your officers is about twelve-to-eighteen months?" said Laidlaw.

"Again, gentlemen – classified."

"That's a very high turnover, Petrie," said Laidlaw.

"If you say so, sir. But I might add, the stakes have got a lot higher too since the start of the Cold War," said Petrie.

Laidlaw swilled his drink and allowed a faint glower at Petrie,

"But you enjoy the game, Petrie, like to see how it plays out?"

"Unlike my predecessor, I haven't been profligate with my assets," said Petrie.

Petrie drew on the last shags of tobacco and shrugged off his Macintosh. The room began to smell like an Irish snug.

More measures of whiskey were poured.

"We do know once selected, an officer undergoes three weeks of intensive training in Scotland and a psychological evaluation before entering the field? Am I correct?" said Laidlaw.

Another whiskey down like the bottom of a sink.

"Your sources are diligent, sir," said Petrie.

Dewar cleared his throat and leaned forward,

"Em, this *'missing'* case officer of yours - when would they be considered overdue?"

"If we don't hear from him in twenty-four hours, it's likely he's been compromised, Minister," said Petrie.

"Or killed?" said Laidlaw.

"Highly likely," replied Petrie.

Laidlaw and Dewar sat back and stared.

"What happens then – em, next of kin informed?" said Dewar.

"I prefer no next of kin, potential compromise, kidnapping, torture – you get the picture. Personal effects destroyed. Accommodation cleared and cleaned, as if they had never existed, sir,"

"Just like a ghost, Petrie?" said Laidlaw.

"Exactly, sir,"

"If your man in the field doesn't report in over the next few days, we have a candidate that might fit the bill," said Dewar.

He took a small folder and slid it across to Petrie.

"I usually consider recommendations, gentlemen, not take them as read?" said Petrie.

He opened out the file. It was a surveillance photograph of a man of about twenty-five. Square jawed and lean. He was dressed in a polo kit and holding the reins of a sturdy pony.

"*Sebastian Holt?*" said Petrie.

"Holt would fit the bill," said Dewar.

"I'll consider it, sir,"

"Very good. Let's keep it just between the three of us, then, eh?" said Dewar.

He leaned forward again, the whiskey taking hold, he rocked and stared as funereal as a crow,

"There's something we want your department to look at. If Holt is approached, I'll ensure the details are sent on."

"Where can we find him?"

"Cambridge. He teaches small-arms training every Wednesday and Thursday."

"Small-arms training?"

"Cambridge, Petrie," said Dewar.

He made it sound like a dismissal.

Petrie rose and downed the whiskey and draped his coat across his arm.

"A particularly good twelve-year old, thank you," he said

The door was opened, and Petrie strode down the corridor. Harrowby was waiting for him at the elevator,

"May I drop you back sir?"

"No. I'll walk thank you."

Petrie tugged on his raincoat, straightened his hat and ignored the stares of people dressed for the warm spring day as he walked.

FOUR

Sebastian Holt floored his Jaguar XK150 allowing the 3.4 litre engine fine tune on the motorway from his mews in Kensington to Cambridge. In the boot was an army kit bag containing three loaded pistols and ammunition. If the local constabulary stopped him he had a signed permit from the head of London CID and a letter of recommendation from his former regiment, The Somerset Light Infantry. He had reinforced the boot to ensure, that anyone curious enough to find out if anything was worth stealing, would have a time of it. Sullen rain clouds hung over the sun-dappled countryside as the city limits gave way to the flowing gowns, books and a profusion of bicycle traffic of Cambridge. Past the market squares of Silver Street, Holt nudged the car in behind the faculty buildings of Queen's College and found a secluded parking space. The first dense splashes of an April shower thumped off the bonnet.

Broughton-Ware was waiting for him.

"Holt," he said.

"Broughton-Ware,"

"What happened to the Bentley?"

"Sold it."

"Fools and their money, as they say."

"As you so often remind me, *the upper classes do nothing, and they do it rather well.* I thought I'd do something useful," said Holt.

"Your country salutes you, Sebastian," said Broughton-Ware.

He was a tall pencil of a man, thin with the beginnings of a stoop. Unfashionable round glasses caught the sunlight on his long nose and a frayed tweed suit hung on his frame. He smelled of chalk dust.

"The room is set up – the little lass is ready for you."

Broughton-Ware's voice was a deep Pennine growl that could be heard all over the campus and playing fields.

Holt hauled the equipment bag up out of the boot and double-locked it with a special key. He followed Broughton-Ware to a long commons room. They descended a flight of old stone steps to a long concrete cellar beneath. A trestle table stood at one end of the cellar and straw bales at the other. Secured to these were the silhouettes of men with targets circled around key areas; head, torso, stomach.

Standing at the table was a girl.

A loose knitted jumper, slacks and a prim looking pony-tail couldn't disguise just how pretty she was. Doe eyes framed by long lashes and a bee-stung pout gave her a mischievous look. Solid-looking wellington boots added to her ingenue demeanour.

"This is Mr Holt, he'll walk you through this," said Broughton-Ware

"Good morning, you can call me Sebastian if you wish, or Holt,"

"Dorothy Jones and it's just Dorothy, Mr Holt - not Dottie, or Doe, just Dorothy,"

Despite her stern tone and clear emphasis, Dorothy worked a loose strand of mouse coloured hair around her ear.

Holt slung the bag onto the table,

"May I ask where your posting is, Dorothy?"

"Israel, Mr Holt. Tel Aviv. Front desk of a travel agency – Regal Holidays," she replied.

Holt set out three pistols and their corresponding magazine. He always studied the initial reaction to the guns. The men always pounced on them like children at Christmas. Women approached with caution. Her gaze fell on the middle one; a Czech CZ52.

"Good choice," said Holt.

"The others?"

"A Walther PP and a Beretta,"

"Have you a preference, Holt?" she asked.

"Try them all," he said, "they all do the same job if used correctly."

Dorothy produced two wads of cotton wool from a crocodile clutch at her feet and worked them into her ears. Then holding each gun, fired at each target. Head, torso and the groin all took direct hits.

"You're a natural," said Holt.

He took time explaining the mechanics of each gun; how to assemble and reassemble them. He had her clearing the breeches and explained the importance of daily maintenance. As the lesson progressed, Broughton-Ware smoked a roll-up and leafed through an aged leather-bound matins. Holt would make a good teacher, thought Brought-Ware. He wasn't what his wife would call *'a pest'* around a young woman. He explained everything matter-of-factly, as if he were dealing with an equal.

Broughton-Ware knew what had happened in Cairo. He had stood beside Holt at Samantha Barnes' remembrance service at King's College.

Dorothy Jones was quick, eager and settled on the CZ52.

After an hour, the training session was over. Holt filled out the paperwork for the FO and Broughton-Ware counter-signed.

"Good luck with your assignment, Dorothy," said Holt.

He offered his hand. She shook it,

"Goodbye, Holt. Will I be issued with the CZ?"

"Probably."

"I like this one."

"Keep it. I'll ensure you receive two more clips."

"Do you collect guns, Holt?"

"No."

Broughton-Ware gave a cough and closed his precious book,

"Dinner, Holt?"

"Love to."

"There's a smashing pub called The Pickerel, I go there all the time," said Dorothy.

Holt glanced over at Broughton-Ware

"Why not?" he replied.

FIVE

Frank Sinatra was singing about a bar in far Bombay. The vinyl pulsed, crackled and whirled on the powder blue record player. Dorothy Jones pursed her lips as she lit two cigarettes and handed one to Holt. Her university digs were everything he had expected, a bohemian chaos of books, records, unwashed teacups and underwear either undecided on or due for the laundry on the floor. Her smile creased into two perfect dimples,

"So, Holt, tell me about yourself?"

"There's really not too much to tell,"

"Grumpy Broughton-Ware likes you,"

"That's debatable,"

"Born?"

"New Delhi,"

"Parents?"

"Both dead,"

"Good,"

"Good?"

"I don't have to worry myself about meeting them – I'm sensitive to judgement – would they have judged me?"

"Probably,"

Dorothy Jones stretched out. The early morning sunshine shimmered on her naked skin. She was perfectly proportioned, she reminded Holt of Marilyn Monroe.

"Did you like India?" she asked.

"Loved it."

"Miss it?"

"No,"

Holt eyes darkened as he smoked.

"My father committed suicide, a lot of shame to carry,"

"I'm sorry, your mother?"

"Cancer."

"We all have our crosses, Holt,"

Dorothy Jones back-tracked,

"All Maharajas, polo, cricket and parties, then?" she asked.

"Endless, Miss Jones, endless,"

"All perfectly colonial?"

Holt eased up to her and started planting soft kisses under her throat. Her skin smelt of scent and fresh sweat. Her hair fell about her face forming a perfect frame.

"Well, you're certainly keen, Mr Holt," she grinned

He was aroused.

"Then we'd best be careful," he murmured.

"Remember, Sebastian, you owe me two extra clips for my pistol."

Dorothy Jones eased her smooth, exquisite curves into Holt's broad shoulders and her mouth kissed him, thrilling to his slow caresses,

"Do you seduce all your teachers, Miss Jones?" asked Holt.

"Only the ones I like."

"You will be careful out there?"

"Of course, Sebastian."

"Beware of strongboxes?"

"Strongboxes?"

"Never mind, Miss Jones."

"Call me Dorothy,"

"Later,"

She straddled him working her hips slowly up and down him. Bending forward, the tips of her cold breasts brushed his skin. Her mouth was warm and willing. She eased herself onto him and wrapped her legs around his hips.

Ole Blue Eyes skipped and clipped as the record spun to a close. Holt and Jones rolled about on top of her tiny bed. They tumbled out, demolishing her night stand and sending the needle across the vinyl grooves with a cry.

SIX

Cambridge

"My name is Caxton Petrie."

Broughton-Ware's home was a rambling Elizabethan country house in the town of Ely. It had a collapsed-looking appearance of untamed shrubs, ancient brickwork and derelict stables. The kitchen though, was Broughton-Ware's canvas. No restaurant in Piccadilly, Paris or Manhattan could meet his meticulous, exacting standards. Every pot, pan and plate gleamed, and the immense oven and hob glowed like a blacksmith's forge. He poured a generous red for Petrie and Holt to accompany his roast with all the trimmings.

"Sebastian Holt."

Holt didn't proffer a hand. He'd seen Petrie's type at his father's funeral. The inevitable British civil servant, bland and grey, obstinate and dutiful. He eyed the suit; it was an expensive cut, bespoke and exact. Caxton Petrie had standards.

"This is excellent, Broughton-Ware, excellent, the lamb simply melts in your mouth," said Petrie.

Broughton-Ware seemed to stand to full attention, a wisp of a smile appeared.

"The garlic and rosemary help, I think," he said.

"Yes, I quite agree, how's yours?"

Petrie stabbed a skewered piece of lamb in the direction of Holt's portion.

"Very, good, Mr Petrie. I think Broughton-Ware missed his calling."

Broughton-Ware pulled up a chair to the linen draped table and pinched a few grains of crusty salt over the roast.

"Though the '55 is still a little young," said Petrie.

He swilled the wine around in a crystal-cut glass.

"Perhaps it needs a little time to breathe?" said Holt.

"Indeed. Or decanted. I'll get to the point, if I may?"

Petrie placed the silver service side-by-side the Belfast linen napkins.

"I'd be grateful," replied Holt.

"Broughton-Ware is an old colleague of mine. We belonged to the same... club at one point, I suppose?"

He glanced at Broughton-Ware.

"MI6?" asked Holt.

"Yes," replied Petrie, "MI6, though closer to the Middle East Desk, Transjordan, Iraq and Israel; that general area. I represent a discreet branch of the organisation,"

"...and?" asked Holt

"I'd like to make you an offer,"

"Offer?"

"Offer, yes, an offer – this really is good, Broughton-Ware."

"My pleasure, Petrie, more wine?"

"Yes please, thank you,"

"What sort of offer?" asked Holt.

"I'd like you to make a few enquiries. Discreet enquiries."

"Enquiries?" said Holt.

Holt rose and went to the marble island in the middle of the kitchen. Taking a carving knife, he sliced through the roast. The meat bowed and fanned onto the plate.

"A few days abroad, Holt, nothing too exciting. I see you have an excellent service record, so you can be trusted. You're a very wealthy man but not reckless with cash. No outstanding gambling debts, no peccadilloes that could leave you exposed to blackmail or worse," said Petrie.

Holt slid back onto his chair and chewed as Petrie continued,

"A spy?" said Holt.

"Not exactly," said Petrie.

"Then what, exactly?"

"A representative," said Broughton Ware.

Holt glanced over,

"Ah, my alma-mater, The Empress of India Thread Company?"

"Passport, airline tickets and a Hotel booking, all arranged – a BOAC from London to Paris, tomorrow afternoon."

"My car?"

"Leave it here. I'll arrange a ministry car, and you'll pass through customs and passport control without having to queue."

"Your name will be Richard Ives; a mid-level business executive," said Broughton-Ware.

"The Empress of India Thread Company's my family's business, on my mother's side,"

"I'm sorry she passed so young," said Petrie.

"I'm sure you are. Why, may I ask, do you think I would be interested?"

Broughton-Ware glanced over the rim of his unfashionable glasses to Petrie. He chewed with a cautious dab of a napkin around his mouth. Holt detected the faint smile beginning again.

"You won't be expected. Most agents, operatives – spies, if you will, come from the academic pool; Eton, Cambridge, Oxford – a pool merrily infiltrated by the Russians since the 1930's. You, on the other hand would be harder for the other side to spot – privately educated, no English academic record but would fit right at home at embassy or diplomatic level," said Petrie.

Petrie started into his meal again. He ate as if every bite oiled the gears of his brain, his voice, though cultured and mellowed by tobacco, had a Scottish burr,

"The Americans have 'lost' an operative – an agent codenamed *'Cochise'*. Being Americans, they'll upset everything like a tizzy bull in a china shop, so we've suggested we try to find him first. If we can locate and better yet, return 'Cochise' intact, it'll improve our somewhat shaky standing with the CIA."

Holt sipped the wine. He thought of Dorothy Jones, on her jaunty way to Tel Aviv. He looked around Broughton-Ware's cosy fragrant dungeon of hanging copper pots and pans.

"I'll have to inform the board of directors. Let them know I'm travelling," said Holt

"Already done, through the India desk, we still have a few friendly connections over there," said Petrie.

A surge of a car headlights outside meant Broughton-Ware's wife, Eleanor had finished her day's teaching at the nearby girl's school.

They had no children.

Holt took the thick manila envelope and leafed through its contents,

"How did you get my photograph?" he asked.

A black and white image of Holt stared out of the passport with grim determination,

"We used an MI5 surveillance shot last month at Windsor, courtesy of the Royal Protection Unit. Your polo team won the tournament I believe?" replied Petrie

"Lovely," said Holt.

Richard Ives. A letter of introduction beneath the letterhead was in French and English. BOAC tickets and the chit confirming a modest hotel booking in Montmartre all lay on the table.

"I'm assuming your private tutor taught you the language?"

"He did," replied Holt.

"Fluent?"

"Yes," said Holt.

"Even better. Richard Ives – are you ready?"

"If I may, Mr. Petrie, I'd like to make a few amendments? You did make several assumptions and frankly, I don't like them."

"By all means," replied Petrie.

His eyes had taken on a flinty light.

"Just an enquiry?" said Holt.

"You'll be a week at most," replied Petrie.

Holt drained the last of the wine,

"You were right, Mr. Petrie, the vintage is a little young," he said.

"If it's allowed time to breathe, who knows how it will turn out?"

"Okay, I'll do it," said Holt.

He poured another generous measure from the bottle.

"Very good, Holt," said Petrie.

SEVEN

Paris

Holt's eye was drawn to Le Monde's headline – '***La République est morte!***'. It was yesterday's edition, left folded on the table of the café. He opened it out and glanced through the column print. Gaillards's Fourth Republic seemed to be all sex scandals, drugs and financial corruption. The Algerian War wasn't showing any signs of letting up either and the French army there was racking up defeats at the hands of 'savages'.

The café noir arrived, and Holt settled back to watch the Hotel de la Louisiane from across the street. Petrie had said it was the last place *'Cochise'* had been seen; possibly booked in under a different name. It was situated in a perfect location, the Rue de Seine gave one access to Jardin du Luxembourg, and streets that radiated out towards multiple metro stations. If you had to escape, this was the perfect place to start. The hotel's facade had a crumpled charm, a place to find a bohemian gentleman of leisure rather than an absconded American agent. The city of Paris walked, cycled and drove in all its early morning élan past his table.

He read the paper. He re-read it and then worked from back to front. Petrie was right; spying was a waiting game. He smoked two cigarettes and ordered another coffee. If there was a next time, he'd bring along a book. Holt finished the coffee and tipped the waiter.

Folding the newspaper, he walked toward the hotel.

Holt removed his sunglasses in the hotel's foyer. He hadn't a plan as such, just make an enquiry at the man's last known abode, written down on a slip of paper by Petrie.

"Can I help you, sir?" asked the concierge, his handsome features and sallow colouring hinted at North African.

"Hi, yes, hello. Yes. I'm looking for an old acquaintance, an American gentleman I met in London a week ago. My name is Ives, Richard Ives."

The concierge shrugged.

"I don't recall an American businessman. Sorry,"

"That is a pity, I was hoping to catch up. Social call really,"

"No American stayed here,"

"Recently? Last week perhaps?"

"Non,"

The concierge began leafing through a magazine. He was finished dealing with Holt.

"I've a few colleagues in the city visiting for the next few days, has anyone else been looking for him?"

"You are the first, Monsieur. But again, no American staying here,"

"Well that is something – definitely no Americans staying here?"

"No American, Americans. Au revoir."

"Sorry for inconveniencing you,"

The concierge turned another page. He didn't look up.

Holt knew he was lying. He had cash, but that was no guarantee of a truthful answer. Cash would start a paper trail and Holt wanted to be discreet. He looked around the foyer and was thinking of his next tack when a young woman strode in. She had an orange patterned headscarf and dark glasses that framed her slightly wide features. Not classically beautiful, she was dressed in a stylish striped roll neck and black pleated slacks. A striped handbag of white, blue and orange that had seen better days hung from her arm. Her pumps finished off the appearance of an aspiring drama student,

"There you are, darling!" she said.

Her accent had the drawling cadences of southern France, the languid Mediterranean.

She took Holt's hand,

"I'm sorry for my fiancé's persistence, he's got the wrong hotel – darling, I've been searching for you everywhere, come on, we're late!"

She peered over the sunglasses rim. Holt didn't need telling twice. Her gaze was cold, professional and all kinds of urgent.

What threw him was how she still managed to squeeze a pout into her fixed smile.

"We have to go, *Cherie*, now,"

Her grip was strong, despite her slight frame.

Holt gave the concierge a smile and allowed himself to be led out of the hotel.

"Who are you?" he asked

"Not now."

She tugged him across the street and manoeuvred him to another table at the café. Before he could speak, she leaned across and kissed him on the lips. Her mouth was warm. She tasted of menthol cigarettes and her scent was delicate. He began to bend into the kiss as she ran a lingering finger through his hair.

The screech of brakes made him glance over to the Hotel de la Louisiane. Two black cars had pulled up outside of it. Big blocky cars. Russian cars.

Men got out. Men in uniform black suits, white shirts and pencil ties. Two positioned themselves at either side of the hotel doors while the rest of them poured in.

"KGB," said the girl.

"You or them?"

"Them. You're not staring over. Good."

"I'm enjoying the view here. Gendarmes?"

"Always late,"

"My name is Richard Ives,"

"We know who you are, Monsieur Holt. Tell me you didn't hand him a business card?"

"No."

"Cash - dollars, francs?"

"No."

"Give a name?"

"Richard Ives,"

"He might forget."

In less than a minute the men had returned to the vehicles. Between two of them limped the hapless concierge.

"Not good," said the girl.

She clicked her tongue and murmured, "Merde".

She removed her glasses, her eyes were a deep, piercing blue,

"Car?"

"Metro," replied Holt

"We have to leave now. I have a motorcycle,"

"Look, Miss, I'm hardly going to charge off somewhere with a stranger."

"You paid for your own flight – BOAC first class, you didn't have a lunch, but you ordered a Bordeaux '51. You drank two black coffees and purchased a carton of 20's cigarettes. You have one item of luggage, an Italian leather duffel bag. SDECE. I'm…"

"I know, SDECE is the French Secret Service, do you have a name?"

"Aubuchon,"

"First or last?"

"Just Aubuchon, Monsieur,"

"Aubuchon,"

Across the street, one of the men stood panning the café. His beard was a red pastiche of Lenin, he looked sickly pale with wire-frame glasses. His gaze fixed on the girl.

"We have to move. Now," she said.

The man with the red goatee was looking left and right before stepping off the kerb. He was reaching into his breast pocket with one hand. The other was motioning his comrades to follow him.

Holt and the girl began to run.

They dashed down a side street, Aubuchon was fast. She had an urchin's ability to side-step, dodge and slink around the morning pedestrians. She wasn't afraid to sling the handbag either. Holt kept up. They came to a long line of parked scooters and bicycles. She hopped onto a Peugeot, a bulky S.57B,

"Ride pillion?" she said.

She wrapped her bag around the handlebars and turned the ignition key and pressed the starter.

"If necessary," replied Holt.

She twisted the throttle. The machine responded with a hearty buzz.

"Your hotel?"

Holt had to shout over the engine's din.

"I thought I'd avoid all that – The Chantilly Polo Club, - Rue de Verneuil,"

"Could you pick anywhere farther?"

"I wasn't expecting you."

Aubuchon opened the throttle and Holt placed his hands under the small, but well upholstered pillion seat.

"I just saved your life, Monsieur,"

"I'm eternally grateful."

The sturdy little Peugeot rattled out of the side street and merged with the hundreds of other scooters, bicycles and cars.

Aubuchon's headscarf flapped as they pitched and swerved away from the street where The Hotel de la Louisiane was now no longer an option.

*

Ostrovsky stood on the pavement as a man and a French agent in an orange headscarf disappeared around the street corner. Glancing along the tables of the restaurant he regarded the clientele with revulsion and regret. He would have had no compunction in slaying the girl in broad daylight and removed one more enemy agent on the list provided by Sukhachen, but the man with her was unexpected. He loosened his grip on the small snub-nosed gun devised by his superiors; the same size as a cigarette case with three poisoned bullets. One would be enough to kill instantly. He turned on his heel and plodded back to the car. He got into the back seat where the terrified concierge sat. The concierge's nose was broken and streaming blood down through his pencil moustache. Both eyes were swollen shut and his upper lip was busted apart.

He was crying. His hands were fastened behind his back in handcuffs.

The driver handed the hotel's guest book over to Ostrovsky,

"We have a few questions for you," said Ostrovsky, "We'll go through this line by line,"

To the terrified concierge, Ostrovsky's leaden French sounded like a whetstone.

The two black Russian cars swung out and accelerated away towards the outskirts of Paris, returning to the location where they could take their time extracting the information they needed.

EIGHT

Aubuchon idled the scooter and looked back at Holt.

"Here?"

"Here,"

At the edge of Trois-Forêts, the Chantilly Polo Club was an imposing seventeenth century chateau. Playing grounds and ornamental gardens were framed by an impressive moat. The coat of arms, emblazoned with horses, gave the imposing building a medieval aspect. The distant clack and applause of a polo game drifted toward them on the warm breeze. Aubuchon's scooter was as diminutive as a gnat along the immense and well-tended gravel drive and the pulsing octagonal fountain,

"Now we can talk," said Aubuchon.

She rolled her shoulders forwards and back to unlock the strained muscles from the scooter.

"You need to leave," she said.

"Leave?"

"Leave. Yes. Leave. This isn't your remit, Monsieur Holt,"

Holt looked around, they were alone.

"I was asked to enquire discreetly,"

"About an American, I know," she replied.

"He's gone missing?"

"We will find him. Go home. Go back to your life, you don't belong here."

"I have a phone and a teletype set up here. All I'm going to do is confirm that I visited his last known abode and he is no longer there. It might be enough, or I might receive further instructions."

He looked up at the impressive entrance and began pushing the scooter the last hundred yards to the stone vaulted entrance.

"You're out of your depth, Holt. You exposed me by wandering into that hotel."

"A change of hair colour, a little 'lippy',"

She strode in front of him and made him stop.

"Are you serious?"

Holt thought if she was a pool, it would be a deep, dark one with contrasting ripples and swirls. A pool a man could drown in.

"I apologise, no really I do. Thank you for the lift, I'll arrange your petrol and compensate you for any expenses incurred," he said.

She turned on her heel.

Holt pushed the scooter through the unyielding gravel.

Standing at the entrance was a handsome man, dressed in polo colours, battered-looking knee pads and polished riding boots. His smile lit up his handsome features,

"Miss Aubuchon, allow me to introduce you to Rohit Naj. My good friend and confidante,"

"Enchante, Mademoiselle,"

Naj offered to wheel the Peugeot to the garage along the gravel way.

"Monsieur Holt is doing a good job. Is it far?"

"Just around the corner," replied Naj.

"Pity," said Aubuchon.

"What brings you to Paris, Sebastian?"

"A missing man," said Holt.

"A mystery then?" said Naj.

"A dead end," replied Holt.

"Monsieur Holt here just undid a month's work,"

"That is a dead end," said Naj.

The trio and the scooter ambled towards the far side of the club.

"I got your message, Sebastian. I have your rooms booked above the livery yard. Very discreet and perfect timing - lunch is almost ready."

He had the relaxed charm of a pampered existence.

"Thanks, Naj – Has the teletype been installed and connected?"

"Yes, a few questions from the Calcutta offices, but we smoothed it over,"

They found the garage and pushed the scooter into a sheltered alcove.

"I'm starving - will formal attire be necessary?" asked Holt.

"As you well know, for you, Sebastian, the rules don't apply,"

Aubuchon unwound her handbag from the handle bars,

"I always keep a change on stand-by. Give me a minute - is there a place I can freshen up?"

"Miss Aubuchon appears to be always ready…" began Holt.

"Because she's a journalist, Holt. I've read her articles, very insightful," said Naj.

"Thank you," said Aubuchon as she spotted the facilities.

She strode past lolling horses and riders as if she belonged in the court of Louis XVI.

*

"Sebastian had a Manipuri pony, Ayesha, a gift for his twelfth birthday," said Naj.

Aubuchon's transformation; neat little black dress, orange headscarf now wrapped around her slender neck and thick sandy-blonde tresses pinned up was nothing short of spectacular. She had given her eyes a touch of mascara and a dab of lipstick. A crumpled packet of Gauloises lay beside the saucer with a matchbook for a Jazz club perched on top.

"On the morning after India became independent, his father shot it. Lieutenant-Colonel Holt was very drunk, so the first shot grazed her left eye. She bolted. He followed. My father's house was in the next town and he spotted her and caught hold of her reins. Sebastian and his father arrived in a general staff car and after several drunken shots later, leaves poor Ayesha in considerable distress. He forced Sebastian to hold the reins. My father had to take the revolver and put the poor animal out of its misery. That's how I met Sebastian,"

"That's awful. Why?"

"None of the members of the Calcutta Club wanted their horses handed over to pull carts by the lower castes. The British slaughtered all of their polo horses that night."

Holt entered the restaurant and watched the polo game for a moment.

"His father was a brilliant player. Sebastian has followed in his footsteps," said Naj.

Aubuchon hadn't had a good chance to look at Holt. He had changed into an open white shirt, pleated slacks and loafers. He was handsome, though not yet grown into his looks. A Rolex Tudor glinted on his wrist which made him both assured and obscene like the club and its clientele. She thought if he was hers, she'd make him wear something less ostentatious. He was a combination of strength and sensitivity, but his intelligence made him look capable of cruelty. He was a man who walking into a room could make friends and enemies in an instant. A man capable of bringing the worst out of a lover.

He looked over and their eyes locked. He smiled for her and her alone.

She liked that.

His gaze never left as he approached.

"You look absolutely stunning, Miss Aubuchon," he said,

"Thank you, Holt,"

"Sebastian,"

"Sebastian. Rohit was telling me about how you met?"

Holt's expression shifted, his jaw muscles clenched. He reached for the small menu card,

"Poor Ayesha, she didn't deserve that end. Some good came out of it though, I made a good friend."

Naj gave an easy smile and patted Holt's arm.

"Working for Sebastian's family business saved me from pursuing a life of indolent pleasures,"

"His father was a Maharaja," said Holt.

"Oh, when he said house, I thought he meant *house*?" said Aubuchon.

"A house with a fleet of elephants, servants and thousands of hectares of jungle with roaming tigers. Old Rohit here is a prince of Rajputana," said Holt.

The flash of pain had passed. Holt leaned back in his chair and glanced down the menu card.

"So, Miss Aubuchon, what story are you chasing down? Another salacious scandal?" asked Naj.

"Him," nodded Aubuchon.

At a far table was a man dining alone.

"Julius Lanzmann?" said Naj.

Aubuchon's profile was framed by a loose strand of hair, her nose delicately Gallic led to a tender mouth. She blew smoke from the corner of it and then pursed her lips in concentration.

She had a faint acne scar along her jawline. Her plain black dress revealing tanned arms and delicate wrists had an innate ennui. Her eyes though, were pools of intense light. If they were the mirrors to the soul, thought Holt, at this moment in time, it was place filled with fury.

"The *'saviour of the republic',*" said Aubuchon.

The man sat dining alone. He had a large table to himself with a quarter bottle of champagne. In his late forties, he had a perma-tan more as the result of a lamp than outdoors, reworked teeth and a square jaw that had the beginnings of a dewlap.

"A very dangerous man," said Aubuchon, "A charming psychopath without any moral inclinations,"

Without warning, she was up from the table as the waiter arrived,

"Will we order for her?" asked Naj.

"I think we may be leaving," replied Holt.

Aubuchon's slight frame did its best to tower over the man who had placed his knife and fork down with slow deliberation. Her voice carried across the tables in staccato bursts.

So much for discretion, thought Holt.

The man barked back at her, their row now a private affair played out to wary glances and concentrated dining at the tables. He stood and called her a *'Whore like her mother,'* and made a snipping gesture about his head with two fingers,

"Time to leave, Naj. I'll go get her," said Holt.

He took his time getting up, allowing Lanzmann to see him coming.

If he was looking for effect, he was disappointed.

The diners increased their focussed vivacity as Holt drew nearer. From the corner of his eye he could see waiters in their striped waistcoats, barmen and the polished maître 'd beginning to converge.

He stood beside Aubuchon,

"We've interrupted your lunch, I must apologise," he said.

"There is nothing more insulting to a Frenchman as an Englishman trying to speak his language,"

Holt noticed the slight sliver of drool on Lanzmann's lower lip.

"I was born in India." he replied.

"A colonial then, with his pet monkey sitting with him," said Lanzmann.

He glowered over at Naj.

"This club's standards are slipping; he isn't suitably attired," said Lanzmann.

"That 'monkey' you refer to is my close friend, and an extraordinary polo player – do you play?" asked Holt.

"No."

"Are you a member?"

"No. Not yet."

"I could arrange it?"

Aubuchon whirled around and stared at Holt.

"*Arrange* it?" replied Lanzmann.

"But you would need your own horse. Though judging by your meal here, it'd have to be over eighteen hands. A cart horse, a dray, probably, Monsieur,"

To Holt, Lanzmann's smile reminded him of a slow-burning fuse wending its way through undergrowth to several tons of high explosive. His bespoke suit, French cuffs and silk pocket square offset the impressive ruby that sat like a bullet wound in the silver tie clasp. He was in corpulent, manicured middle age and yet still had a waft of the gutter about him; packing crates and wharf-side boxes that hung about him like a faint whiff of sulphur.

"This woman has been spreading lies. Lies and innuendo. The newspapers spew her falsehoods."

"We're leaving now. Again, I must apologise. Send your bill over to me and I'll pay for it, Monsieur,"

"Is she your lover?"

"No."

"You should beat her. Take her as a lover and beat her often, fix that lying mouth of hers,"

Before Aubuchon could launch herself across the table, Holt took her hand. He squeezed it.

"I was raised to respect a lady. I really think you should apologise," said Holt.

"I will not. Now leave."

"Leave me the bill and enjoy a bottle of champagne on me,"

"I don't want anything from you or your whore, go away. Now."

Holt turned them away.

"Well that went well," he said.

"Vive la Republique!" shouted Aubuchon back at Lanzmann.

Lanzmann stared at her for a moment and then shrugged, returning to his meal.

"What was that finger gesture he made?" asked Holt,

"My mother was shorn in a public square for collaborating with the Nazi's," said Aubuchon, "I was a child when the Germans arrived. Her husband was dead, she took a lover and she raised me by herself,"

"I'm sorry," said Holt.

"Don't be. I'm not."

Naj pulled a chair back and seated Aubuchon.

"We should leave, Sebastian, we're drawing attention," murmured Naj.

"Not at all, Naj, not now - I'm ordering the poached egg, artichoke and pleurottes. I think a bottle of Le Monrachet should do the trick," said Holt.

Holt held Lanzmann's stare as he glowered over at them. Lanzmann ate mechanically. The man is unstable, thought Holt.

Holt raised a glass.

Lanzmann returned his attention to his meal.

"I'll have the chocolate mousse then, Sebastian," said Naj.

"I'll just have the coffee," said Aubuchon.

They dined amid the rapacious and the unscrupulous, the grandees, the politicians and priests, the old money, the new money, the once monied and the titled to the clack and whump of the Polo games beyond. A sullen man sat alone with a repellent aura of power emanating from his pores – Julius Lanzmann, the saviour of France. He clicked his fingers and the fawning waiters cleared his table. A dessert cart and cheese board appeared and a box of expensive cigars. Lanzmann perused the cart and selected a thick chocolate cake. His moment of pleasure interrupted by a tall, lean man striding into the restaurant and bending like a coat hanger wire to whisper into his master's ear,

"Personal security detail," said Aubuchon, "paid by our taxes,"

Lanzmann rose and shook out his napkin and cracked it into a fold and tossed it onto the table. He put an arm around the man as he left, whispering in his ear. The air in the room lifted and clinked with bon homie.

Holt dwelt on the situation and thought it a dead end. He'd send a report to Petrie at Whitehall, compensate Aubuchon and return her to the city, play a few chuckkas with Naj and fly home.

"I think it's time I checked in with my uncle," said Holt.

NINE

London

Laidlaw and Dewar dined every Saturday evening at The Saville Club on Brooke Street. Caxton Petrie alighted from the taxi and handed his overcoat to the attendant. He would have preferred the solitude of his rose garden along the Thames, but a phone call Friday evening from Laidlaw's personal secretary had put paid to that.

He found the two men ensconced in red leather studded chairs.

"Ah, Petrie, nice of you to join us, pull up a pew, there's a good fellow," said Laidlaw.

He had changed from his subdued pinstripe to flannel slacks, plain shirt and an old school tie that had seen better days. Dewar seemed to have slept in his suit.

"The pheasant is really quite excellent," said Laidlaw.

Petrie was proffered a chair by a waiter. All around in small knots were men dining, drinking from the copious bar and murmuring in cloistered tones.

"Whiskey-old fashioned, thank you," said Petrie,

"Em…, you have no objection…?" said Dewar motioning towards his meal.

"No, not at all," said Petrie

"This pheasant alone is worth the trip. What have you got there, Dewar?"

"Salmon, I think. Em, yes, I believe it *is* salmon, Laidlaw,"

"Splendid," said Laidlaw, "The salmon here is excellent. The trout isn't too bad either, though they tend to over-do it,"

"A tricky fish, trout," said Dewar.

"Very tricky indeed," nodded Laidlaw.

He turned his ruddy cheeks to Petrie,

"Our cousins across the Atlantic are making enquiries - our man Holt, how is he doing?"

"I received word from him in Paris yesterday."

"Paris?" said Laidlaw.

"Yes, Paris. The Hotel de la Louisiane. He's drawn a blank there," said Petrie.

Dewar crooked an aged eyebrow, "So *'Cochise'* was there?"

"The Russians seem to think so," said Petrie.

"Russians?" asked Laidlaw.

He glanced around the room and his chewing had increased. Gravy seemed to defeat him at every bite.

"Russians. KGB. French intelligence indicated as such," said Petrie.

"I wouldn't call that a blank then?" said Dewar.

"The concierge was abducted in broad daylight. He's missing," said Petrie.

"Your other agent we discussed, last week, the one who hadn't checked in? Your third cog in the wheel so to speak?" asked Laidlaw

"Killed. We received confirmation last evening."

"Unfortunate – How?"

"Throat cut. Beirut," said Petrie.

"Dashed bad luck, Petrie. So… our man, Holt is still in play, then?" said Dewar.

Both men were absorbed with their meal and the crystal-cut decanter of brandy that glowed deep amber in the light. Petrie's whiskey arrived with a jagged cut of orange peel across its rim. Ten years of rationing hadn't impacted on The Saville Club. Petrie sipped the bitter warmth as he spoke,

"He's flying back, called it a day. The French will find *'Cochise'*, bring him in. One thing though did pop up though – a name; Julius Lanzmann?"

Petrie allowed the plates to be cleared, the glasses to be refilled and the awkward tick of the clock over the fireplace to fill the silence.

A box of cigars, Havana Queens, lined up in tidy rows was placed on the table along with a silver pot of coffee. Petrie regarded his reflection in the silver,

"Lanzmann, a French businessman. Ruby dealer and broker with offices in Tel Aviv. The Andaman Ruby Corporation. Recently took Israeli citizenship. Might be as our cousins across the Atlantic would say - a person of interest."

"Why?" asked Laidlaw.

"He's calling himself *'The saviour of France'*," said Petrie.

"These cigars are excellent, coffee, Petrie?"

The pot shook slightly as Laidlaw poured.

"Dessert?"

"No, thank you,"

"Well, see if you can persuade Holt to stay on a few days. Paris is beautiful this time of year."

"Pretty girls," said Dewar.

"Such pretty girls," replied Laidlaw.

The newspapers arrived, handed out in crisp ironed folds. Laidlaw and Dewar immersed themselves and Petrie flicked to the sports pages – they were the only truths he would accept today. Once he had read the round-up of cricket scores, football results and the race card for Wetherby on Monday, he downed his whiskey and finished his coffee,

"Keep us posted, em, as to how your man is getting along?" said Dewar from behind the wall of paper,

"Yes, Petrie, keep us posted – *bonne nuit*," said Laidlaw.

Petrie donned his raincoat and had a taxi waiting for him as he descended the steps. Big Ben tolled the hour and Petrie climbed into the back of the taxi.

He decided to return to his offices – his rose bushes would have to fend for themselves for another weekend.

TEN

PARIS - Nanterre

The Concierge had been beaten. Beaten repeatedly. He lay on the cold kitchen linoleum. Most of the apartments on the block were still unoccupied, but the uppermost floors had been bought by Department 5 of the KGB. They smelled of fresh concrete, blood and old faeces. In the apartment, all the windows had been sealed and the curtains drawn. The concierge was unconscious. A large table and an immense steel water tank were situated in another room. He was dragged in.

Natalia Kvashnin was waiting. Ostrovsky was repelled and yet fascinated by her nakedness. She wore old scrubbed leather gloves to her elbows, a battered leather hat, like a swimming cap, confining her wild hair and finished off with leather jack boots. Her fair skin though was a canvas of prison tattoos. Only her face had been spared the ink. Across the top of each broad shoulder was etched an eagle with two skulls in each talon. The length of either arm was a flowing barbed wire interwoven with hammers and guns in faded blue. On either breast, two-headed eagles touched wings across a plough and sickle framed by the red star on the powerful chest bone between them. Her pubis was shaved, and the flesh was etched with a weeping red heart crying viscous black blood onto her powerful thighs. On either thigh, ornate Asian eyes stared out unblinking crying long tears to the stars etched onto her knee caps. Across her body were images of broken swastikas, inverted crucifixes, images of Lenin and Stalin with halos and when she turned, her back was an immense lattice-work of scars, weal's and huge black death's head biting down on an iconised Madonna and child. Each solid buttock for once showed a sign of femininity; detailed mimosas of red and yellow – Stalin's favourite flower. The back of each thigh had skulls in profile smoking cigars and smiling toward each other in knowing satisfaction.

The concierge was dragged by his heels into the room and stripped naked with a cloth shears. The bloodied rags were dumped into a large sack for disposal later. The concierge's handcuffs were removed, he was hoisted and tossed onto the long table. Then Natalia set to work. From the vat she pulled long strips of wet canvas. With assured strength starting from his head she mummified him in the cold material. His limp form was turned and rotated and within an hour only his hands and shattered mouth were exposed. Natalia wiped a rivulet of sweat from her amber eyes and then squatted down leaning in, listening for a breath,

"Now, we wait, comrades," she said, "turn up the radiators,"

As the room heated up, the canvas began to dry out and constrict. Reaching into her kit bag, she pulled out a metal box. Inside were long blackened metal skewers of varying lengths. She lined them along the edges of an electric hot plate wired up beside the table. She pulled out heavy industrial welder's gloves and placed them beside them. Standing up, she dismissed Ostrovsky's two KGB companions,

"We will take it from here, comrades. Leave."

They skulked from her amber gaze with jackets draped over rolled up bloodied sleeves. Once the front door was closed and locked, Kvashnin turned to Ostrovsky.

"Now, my dangerous little brother Ostrovsky, we shall fuck," she said.

*

The black Russian cars glided out of the suburbs, passing Julius Lanzmann's Ford Comète Majesty. He read the newspaper hiding his face, shadowed by his fedora; just another businessman rushing around Paris. The car pulled up to the apartment block – uniform and bland, it reminded him of the edifices being thrown up around Tel Aviv for a sudden population that hadn't expected to survive the second world war. Lanzmann's driver opened the rear door,

"Return in two hours," said Lanzmann, tilting his hat over his eyes.

The empty, unfinished projects acted as a wind tunnel for the breeze. Lanzmann dashed ahead of the sudden squall to where a concierge and a hotel guest book lay waiting for dissection. He stood at the doorway and looked around. The site was littered with building materials and equipment, outhouses and shacks all unoccupied were scattered amid pipes and concrete blocks and stanchions of steel. In a few days workers would start their shifts and the whole project would be a hive of activity. The rain abated, and Lanzmann shook the droplets off his cashmere overcoat. Glancing around one more time, he produced a key that opened the front door to the apartment.

ELEVEN

In the end the concierge gave up what they wanted to know. Straddling a kitchen chair, Lanzmann had watched the mummified concierge have heated needles inserted under his fingernails. Constricted by the canvas and shackled to the table, his screams and thrashings reverberated around the room. Lanzmann had also become aware of another smell lingering around, the salty aroma of sex; he stared at the couple, she was as imposing as he was reluctant; their rutting would be a very one-sided affair, he thought.

On either side of the table, they had repeated the same questions over and over. Ostrovsky leafing through the hotel's guest book read each guest's name aloud with Kvashnin repeating. The man's pleas for mercy went unheeded, neither tormentor was feeling generous today. It was hard to know if it was day or night. Time had deadened to a crawl. The heat in the room and the press of the bodies engaged in the torture forced Lanzmann to remove his cashmere coat. He sought a hook around the apartment but found none. He draped the expensive coat across his legs.

"The American?" asked Ostrovsky.

"American?" whispered the concierge.

"Where is he?" asked Ostrovsky.

"Left,"

"Left? Left where, tell me,"

"I don't know,"

"The pain will stop soon, I promise you. Stop. Now think, think, you do remember him, the American?"

The pause was sufficient to allow Ostrovsky a nod. Natalia probed under the nail of the concierge's ring finger with a burning needle.

"His name, what was his name? shall we start again? Is it here? Here in the book?"

The concierge flinched and squirmed under Kvashnin's ministrations. Halfway through the list, he gasped at a name – *Burnett*.

"Bill Burnett? Is that his name?"

Lanzmann leaned forward. Ostrovsky nodded. Kvashnin pulled a heated six-inch needle in her heavy glove. Forcing her weight onto the shackle, she thrust the needle with expert precision deep under the nail of the middle finger.

The mummified figure bounced up and down. The table shook. Lanzmann averted his eyes.

"Bill Burnett?" asked Ostrovsky. He assumed *'Cochise'* had used a false name.

Silence.

Kvashin with a swift flick of the wrist broke the concierge's middle finger.

It was met with a howl.

"Bill Burnett?" said Ostrovsky.

The thumb was next.

Kvashnin delicately replaced a loose strand of ash-coloured hair back under the leather cap. She wiped the beads of perspiration away from her brow, her tattoos shimmering. The amber eyes drifted to Ostrovsky; another fuck on the old mattress in the next room was pending.

Ostrovsky tore off the page with Burnett's name on it.

He tossed the guest book into the sack with the soiled and ragged clothing.

"Now. The man in foyer," he said.

"Man?"

"Yes, the man, In the foyer with the girl,"

"Pretty,"

"Yes, very – did she call him a name?"

"I can't remember. Please, please Monsieur, I have a family, they will be worried..."

Ostrovsky reached for the cloth shears on the floor. He carved rough holes into the canvas where the eyes were.

"The next needles will be going into your eyes. My colleague here is very adept at measured application. The man's name?"

The words flowed in a stream,

"A friend. Acquaintance. Visiting for a few days. So pretty. Fiancé – wrong hotel. Hadn't seen them before. London. Business man. Men..."

"Name?"

"No. please, I can't remember,"

Lanzmann walked out of the room. The sweat was pouring from him. He stood in the kitchen listening to the screams. He walked to the kitchen sink. A lone tooth puddled in blood lay near the plug hole. Lanzmann ran the tap, washing his hands. Cupping them, he splashed water into his face and quaffed handfuls of metallic water. In the room beyond, the screams had died down to wails. He turned to find Ostrovsky wiping a bloodied rag through his fingers,

"Richard Ives. A Richard Ives was looking from him. From London," said Ostrovsky.

"MI6?" said Lanzmann.

"Maybe."

"Bill Burnett, Richard Ives."

"Ives?"

"You saw him?"

"With a French agent."

"Find her, you'll find him. Kill them both."

"Him?" nodded Ostrovsky back towards the room.

"Kill him too. Drop him into the foundations. Guest book too."

Lanzmann walked back into the room. Kvashnin was strangling the mummified concierge. Lanzmann donned his expensive coat and left to the drumming of feet on the table. He descended the stairs two at a time to the driver waiting in the dark. Lanzmann was satisfied. Bill Burnett should be easy to find.

The car sidled out of the construction site. The security man waved them through.

Dollars buy endless security, thought Julius Lanzmann. Endless security and complete discretion.

TWELVE

The taxi pulled up outside the polo grounds. It was a big low-slung Citroën. As the driver showed no compunction to get out,

Holt put his own leather duffel bag into the boot. Aubuchon kept her straw bag fixed to her shoulder. He had offered his apartment to her while he slept on Naj's sofa. Two afternoon chuckkas of polo and the well-sprung but uneven sofa had left Holt's left shoulder in a knotted tangle of pain. Rolling his shoulders forward and back in brisk jerks, he planned to swim in one of the public pools that dotted Paris and then seek out a Turkish bath. Aubuchon had declined the offer of breakfast after he had dialled his apartment three times before she answered.

Holt had dined alone.

He opened the taxi's rear door.

"Thank you, Holt," she said.

"Naj will return your scooter; you're almost out of petrol. He's taken it off to the local garage; thinks there's enough in the tank to get him there. I think he's looking forward to the jaunt back to the city. I told him to park it in the same place?"

"He'd better bring it back in one piece - Airport please," said Aubuchon.

The driver noddcd. An enormous, chewed cigar bobbed up and down amid the five-o'clock shadow.

"Well, it was a pleasure, mademoiselle Aubuchon," said Holt.

She still had her black dress on. He was aware of her legs as the skirt rode up. She pulled the hemline to a primmer length. Lighting one of her Gauloises from her jazz matchbook, she was silhouetted in a wreath of smoke. She smelled of fresh soap.

"Not at all, it was my joy," she said.

She pulled on her sunglasses and leaned back, resting her head.

"What time is your flight?" she asked.

"Change of plan – can you drop the lady off first?" said Holt.

The cigar bobbed 'yes'.

"What change of plan?"

The studied ennui had evaporated. She leant over to him.

"Go home, Holt. I mean it."

"You could lower your voice,"

"He's one of our drivers – isn't that so, Patrice?"

Patrice's cigar dipped once as he started the engine.

"Well, I have to stay on for a few more days," said Holt.

"We'll see about that, Holt."

It was the last thing he remembered.

At a junction along the XIII Arrondssement they were struck side-on by a Renault truck. Holt's mind flashed shards of images through the shroud of darkness; Aubuchon's first glorious smile at a quip. Splintered glass. The interior of the taxi rolling not just over, but forwards too. Crumpling sounds. The cityscape swirling through the collapsing windscreen. His body leaving the seat and thumping around the inward pressing metal. Then everything went black.

Hell is darkness, succour is darkness, he thought. He wondered if there are other kinds of blackness, not just the one he was enduring now. What other kind of darkness was there?

*

Holt opened his swollen eyes. His arms ached. His tongue felt swollen in his mouth. He tried to raise a hand to investigate but his arms were strapped to the arm of a chair. Through searing shots of pain, he raised his head to look around. His trousers were shredded and covered in brown matted blood. His knees felt like firework displays and his ankles sent messages from his torn socks to his brain that something was seriously wrong with them.

He was in a room. More of a long corridor with high windows and curtains of royal blue held in place by golden braids. Above them, an ornate and corniced ceiling with a succession of crystal chandeliers stretched out to wide gilded doors. The walls were lined with paintings that smelled of old linseed, cracked varnish and damp. To his right sat Aubuchon. A glaring cut was slashed across her perfect cheekbone. Her hair was matted with blood. Like him, her arms and legs were fastened to the chair with the same curtain braids. Her chin was resting on her chest. She looked asleep.

Through his narrow vision, Holt became aware of movement in front of him. A dining table was brought in by two people, one a tall woman, the other a diminutive hang-dog version of Lenin. The man from the hotel; thought Holt. The man reaching into an inside pocket where a gun could hide. Both were dressed in olive fatigues. Both were wearing black leather gloves.

A high-backed chair inlaid with gold was placed and Julius Lanzmann walked in and seated himself. He cracked a starched napkin and a young housemaid brought out porcelain, silverware and a large silver tureen. She placed a delicate china bowl of steaming water beside it.

"Thank you, Madeleine."

Lanzmann pulled the lid of the tureen off and with a flourish, began to peel langoustines from their shells,

Madeleine returned with a bottle of champagne in a bucket of ice.

Holt longed for a cool cube of ice to slake his dried-out throat,

"Do you like her, Ives – if that's your name?" said Lanzmann, "I found Madeleine in a forest on the border of Czechoslovakia just after the war, exchanging favours for food. An orphan courtesy of the Germans. She's been in my service ever since,"

He dismissed Madeleine with a wave.

The hang-dog Lenin and the woman hovered either side of Lanzmann, the woman had amber eyes that twinkled with mirth. Her gaze never left Aubuchon,

"You should have fixed her lying mouth like I said," said Lanzmann.

The peeled shells began to stack up on a side plate.

Holt's mouth felt like cotton wool was stuffed into every nook and cranny. His tongue was about to form a word when it discovered a hole where a back molar used to be. He worked himself up to a furious spit and launched a stream of fresh and dried blood onto the luxurious Moorish carpet.

His mouth began to work,

"I'd recommend a Cabernet d'Anjou. Rosé works better with prawns," he said.

Lanzmann gazed at the carpet in suppressed fury. His black eyes and florid complexion matched the shiny pink stack of shells.

The woman stepped out and was across at frightening speed. She struck Holt full force across the temple and he saw a starburst of red followed by a blinding headache.

"Very droll, Monsieur Ives. Langoustines are Norwegian lobster, don't you know?" grinned Lanzmann, "Now you're not *in any position* to arrange anything at The Chantilly Polo Club? Can you? I may need a carthorse, but you're shackled up here with a worthless nag. You are a nobody, a middle level executive. But I am curious, who are you Richard Ives of The Empress of India Thread Company?"

Holt grunted as a new rush of blood filled his mouth; it ran in rivulets down his chin.

The woman with the amber eyes turned her attention to Aubuchon. She ran a lingering finger across Aubuchon's jaw and then the bruised collar bone jutting from the torn black dress. Aubuchon flinched and moaned, pushing herself further into her chair. Her eyes opened, but they were glassy and dazed. The pastiche of Lenin stepped out and stood on the opposite side of Aubuchon.

"Just Richard Ives," said Holt. It sounded muffled and lost as his jaw failed to work. He began working his arms to free them. He ignored Lanzmann's grin and the pain slaloming up his arms.

"I'll be blunt, Monsieur Ives. We've gone through your luggage, your passport, identity papers and letters of introduction," said Lanzmann.

His fished another langouste out the silver tureen and devoured it almost whole.

"These will be on your person, when you are found. I'll keep the watch though, a Rolex I believe? Consider the bill paid. Now - there was a dreadful car accident and a taxi driver is dead. That's all the news that's fit to print," said Lanzmann.

He tossed his soiled napkin on the table and swigged a hearty glass of champagne.

"You'll be a suicide and, for your little whore here, I've something else in mind."

Holt began to focus on Lanzmann's words. They seemed to echo in a distant chamber at the back of his skull. He was dozing in and out of consciousness.

Lanzmann removed something from his pocket. He approached Aubuchon. The man unsheathed a bayonet from his belt. He handed it to Lanzmann. The man and woman held her as the blade glinted. Blackness. Holt opened a lazy eye to see bandages being wrapped around Aubuchon's trembling hand.

Holt tried one last time to knock his chair into them, his legs began to find purchase. He was met with a hearty punch to the chest.

It knocked the wind out of him.

"Your unwelcome arrival, Monsieur has given me a solution to the problem here, a perfect opportunity," said Lanzmann.

He jabbed the bloodied blade toward Aubuchon.

Holt tried to shout her name. He tried to inch toward her.

"Do you know what Aminazin is?" asked Lanzmann, "… this lady is going to administer it."

Holt's movements became more desperate as the woman produced a syringe from a leather pouch secreted on her fatigues.

"It dulls the intellect, destroys emotions and the memory disappears. In a few days' time, this little whore will need to be taught how to read and write again. But, in truth, Ives, the effects are permanent, so a vegetative state is the most likely outcome."

The woman with the amber eyes tapped the needle. Lanzmann gripped a clump of Aubchon's hair and forced her head to her side, exposing the jugular. The man positioned himself in front of Holt and as the blows rained down, the last thing Holt heard before blacking out was Aubuchon's screams.

His last thoughts before oblivion were that there are many, many kinds of darkness. He descended into a new darkness; the borderline of wakefulness and death.

THIRTEEN

Holt gagged up mouthfuls of water. The hazy lights along the dark stone walls told him he was in a river. The stone towpaths beneath the lights told him he was in the Seine. He closed his eyes and allowed his body temperature to even out. Every movement felt like a struggle. Something bumped against him in the dark, giving him a fright. Surfacing, he came face-to-face with the matted hair of Aubuchon. Her complexion in the weak light was wan, he listened for her breath. Treading water, he manoeuvred her around and began to swim toward a bank – any kind of bank with his free arm. The other supported her dead weight. He gagged up the words *'Help', 'Aidez-moi!'* and scanned the walls for a curious face. His entire body felt a strange duality of freezing and being internally ablaze. He let her go for a moment, then gathered himself. She sank. The current was strong, and the undertow was dragging them down. He grabbed her. She was cold. He thought she was dead. Then he spotted a head along the walls. It was big, bald. It turned to listen. It searched. Holt shouted. A second head appeared, dark and glossy. A torch light flashed in his direction. Across the stonework he heard his name repeated. Holt began to kick towards the yelling heads, towing Aubuchon,

"Not far now, Aubuchon. Can you kick?" he said. His teeth were beginning to chatter. The water tasted foul.

"kick dammit, Aubuchon," he said.

He was exhausted and was beginning to let himself go, drift, float. He saw two figures on the bank motioning. One big and bald. The other Naj. They were motioning, beckoning, urging and yelling his name. Holt gave one final kick and succumbed to the cold and pain. He wanted to scream, but the blackness and the weight of water wouldn't allow him that.

*

"My name is Duval" said a voice.

"Amin... ame... zinmen..." murmured Holt.

"Amazing, yes, Monsieur, nothing short of a miracle," said the disembodied voice of Duval.

"Aminazin. Aubuchon. Injected – she was *injected - Aminazin*," said Holt.

"A KGB drug," said Duval.

"They injected her,"

Holt slipped back into darkness.

*

The light had a dishwater quality when he opened his eyes. The grey cropped moon head that gazed back at him was lop-sided, as if one side of the face had decided it had seen enough of the world and wanted to look away. The piercing eyes though, were blue, buried in folds of eyelids framed by unkempt eyebrows. The nose zig-zagged at odd angles. Deep creases on either side of a slit of a mouth suggested an eighty-a-day habit.

"My name is Duval, Monsieur Holt. Alain Duval - SDECE and you, Monsieur, are dead."

"Dead?" said Holt.

"Dead. Drowned. You are a footnote in this morning's newspapers."

"Suicide?"

"Yes. Suicide. Very unfortunate," replied Duval.

The clean sheets and comfortable bed offered little comfort. Holt propped himself up. He was dressed in a loose-fitting gown.

"The girl?"

"Girl?"

"Aubuchon?"

Duval reached into the inner pocket of his suit. Less ill-fitting, it seemed to be struggling to cover the prize-fighter frame. From a large cigarette case he took one and jammed it into Holt's mouth. He lit both with a black Ronson lighter.

"Elsewhere. Safe."

"They injected her."

"We know, you told us. Thank you."

"You'd make a lousy poker player,"

"I don't play poker, Monsieur Holt."

The cigarette was stale. Holt looked around; he was in a dormitory. Lines of beds filled the empty space. A small bedside cabinet had a carafe of water, a bottle of pain killers. Holt became aware too that he was bandaged in places.

"You owe your life to your friend, Naj. He witnessed the taxi collision. It was an army truck. It never stopped. He raised the alarm. Knowing who we're up against, Monsieur Lanzmann, we checked along the river. We found you. Nothing broken. The swellings should go down then you'll be fit to fly home."

"Anything stronger than water here?" asked Holt.

"Coffee?"

"Irish it up will you, Duval?"

"Hennessy?"

"That'll do. Thank you, Alain,"

"Duval."

"Duval,"

Holt lay back on the bed as Duval lumbered from his sight. He closed his eyes and fought back the sudden waves of fear. Not for him, but Aubuchon. He was worried he would never see her again. He closed his eyes and the first images that appeared were the ravaged and dying features of his mother. He remembered her smile and he remembered the watch she'd handed him.

He wanted them both back.

FOURTEEN

"This is a ruby," said Duval.

In Duval's huge fist the stone captured and splintered the sun in hues of crimson. Holt was sitting on a bench in the grounds of the military hospital. Around him, the damaged, the burned, the maimed and mutilated sunned themselves in bandages and casts. Grim doctors in white overcoats hovered like vultures fighting over carrion. Holt's headaches had abated, and he was able to move around without the aid of crutches. That had given him an idea of what it would be like to be an old man.

"It's beautiful," said Holt.

"It was sewn into officer Aubuchon's arm. Expertly sutured too."

"How is she?"

"It was Lanzmann?"

"How is she, Duval?"

"Alive,"

"Authorities? Police?"

"We'll leave them aside for a moment – Lanzmann?"

"Yes."

"He is powerful. Influential."

"So, I gather,"

The precious stone was hypnotic.

"It's a product of The Andaman Ruby Corporation," said Duval.

His voice was deep. The cigarette had a long taper of ash that the breeze snatched at.

"It is an exceptional piece – perfect in colour, cut and clarity. Our experts believe it originated in the Mogok Valley in Burma. The Andaman Ruby Corp., is Lanzmann's source of wealth. His company."

"That's very nice, Duval. But as you said, I'm fit to fly home. I'd like to see miss Aubuchon?" said Holt.

"I'm afraid that's impossible, Monsieur," replied Duval.

"I insist."

"You're not in a position to insist on anything."

"I'd like to pay for her rehabilitation."

"You can, in Tel Aviv."

"Israel?"

"Your government has numerous departments there? A listening station too?"

"I have no idea about my government – I was asked to investigate the whereabouts of someone."

"Cochise?"

"Cochise. Yes."

"His real name is Bill Burnett and he boarded a TWA flight to Tel Aviv a day ago."

"How do you know?"

"The KGB listen to us. We listen to them. It's all very open and courteous. We eavesdropped on an interrogation. We followed up. Of course, if we know he's in Tel Aviv, then the Russians do too. Lanzmann's brokerage for his ruby company is based there."

"Tel Aviv?"

"Richard Ives is dead. No-one will be looking for him, Monsieur."

"Do you have a contact?"

"Levantin Rusev, former Bulgarian intelligence. Useful. Mercenary though. Mossad asset, no doubt playing them off against his former paymasters. You will be flying in to Lod Airport – there's a joint British-Israeli cipher station there. It's located near the town of Lydda."

Holt studied the photograph of Bill Burnett – the moniker suited the rough-hewn features of a western frontiersman. A face, like Duval's, that had seen too much of humanity's darkness.

"What about London?"

"Monsieur Petrie and I are acquainted. He's agreeable," said Duval.

"I bet he is."

"You will need a few days?"

"I can walk, that's enough."

"You leave tomorrow, Monsieur Holt," said Duval.

Holt looked up at the trees and around the grounds. He closed his eyes and inhaled deeply like a man on a tightrope.

"I had clothes?" he said.

"Laundered, cleaned and pressed. No shoes."

"I had a bag?"

"Missing. The taxi was picked clean by the time we got there."

"Passport? Documents?"

"They were on your person – pretty much destroyed. What size shoe are you?"

"A 43, I think."

"I can get you shoes."

Holt looked around the grounds of the veteran's hospital.

"Any of the patients here my suit size?"

"Yes."

"Identification?"

Duval followed Holt's gaze.

"I see what you mean, Monsieur. Yes, you can pose as one of these unfortunate heroes,"

"I hate guns, incidentally."

"I don't see that being a problem. There's a French military transport flying out of Lod one week from today. If you can get Burnett aboard before he's captured, I may allow you to see officer Aubuchon."

"As simple as that?"

"As simple as that, Monsieur."

Holt thought of Aubuchon's smile just before the crash. His thoughts flashed back to their torture. The expressionless actions of Lanzmann, the subtle disconnect of empathy. The studied pleasure of inflicting pain by the man and woman. Lanzmann had erased Aubuchon's smile. Erased her essence. Removed her inner light. He'd rather that she had died fighting than lying in an asylum somewhere.

"What was her first name, Duval?"

"Marianne," replied Duval.

Marianne Aubuchon.

FIFTEEN

Israel

Holt swam. He swam out into the sea and took in a deep breath. He dived into the deep blue, feeling his tired body find its second wind. When his lungs felt close to bursting he ascended, regulating his exhalations. He drifted on the surface.

The sun baked his skin. The salt seeped into his pores. He forgot Paris. He thought about Marianne. His spine began to uncoil from the relentless hours of travel. To his left the millennium-old port of Jaffa bustled with sailing boats. Ahead, the modern concrete and Bauhaus white of Tel Aviv city shone like bone. The azure sky went on for eternity. The beach was dotted with splashes of colour; beach umbrellas, patterned sun loungers. A tanned teenage boy raked the sand and tossed detritus into a sack slung over his shoulder. Standing beside Holt's discarded suit stood Lev Rusev. Rusev raised his arm beckoning him. Holt allowed the tide to nudge him to the shallows and he swam the last few yards. He waded out, the Mediterranean breeze drying him.

Rusev was eating ice-cream from a tub. He had another in his hand. He handed it to Holt. A little wooden spoon drifted in the melted gelato. It cooled Holt's salty mouth. Holt could see his reflection in Rusev's sunglasses. The bruising and swelling had gone down. The eyes were still black and tired looking. He took the glasses off Rusev and put them on.

"How do I look?" he asked.

"Like a movie star. Like Bela Lugosi," said Rusev. His English was heavily accented. It had an ursine timbre.

"That bad?" said Holt.

Rusev nodded. His shock of grey curls spouted beneath his panama hat. He stared out at the sea,

"From here, we are just twenty minutes from Egyptian bombers," he said.

He held his hat above his head as a shade and studied the cloudless sky. His hair was receding at the crown. He reminded Holt of Harpo Marx. He handed Holt a rented vivid green towel from a white shack further down the beach. The shack sold ice-cream too. Holt dressed in his old suit. He felt better now after his flight and drive from Lydda. He had a battered suitcase with a variety of laundered veteran's hand-me-downs. They felt apt. A half-mile walk from the airport had led to the listening station. It had once been a British army barracks. The listening station then confirmed his arrival with Paris and London. He was handed an address and a code-word typed out on a slip of paper. He memorised both and burned the strip in an ashtray. Rusev arrived in a little white Italian car. On the main highway they had passed Ottoman domed police stations, a solitary modern telephone box, orchards and nut-brown girls in combat fatigues with their caps tilted in modish angles. A train had flashed past on glittering silver rails.

"They arrive every day by sea; on any kind of ship. They get the train from Jaffa to Tel Aviv. Every day. The city will burst one day, my friend," said Rusev.

"Who?" asked Holt.

"The Jews – we run from where we are no longer wanted," said Rusev.

A toothless old Arab had peered curiously into the car when they had stopped at a dusty crossroads. He had squinted in, refused the lift offered and shuffled on. Then on the long sweeping drive toward the city, Holt had spotted the sea.

He needed to swim; the blue had looked inviting.

"My hotel?" asked Holt.

"The Jephfra. It's nice," said Rusev.

"Bed bugs?"

"Every hotel in the city has bugs – KGB, Mossad, CIA, MI6 – which are you?"

"None. Just doing a spot of sight-seeing," said Holt.

"That's not what the French say. You're looking for an American?"

"Yes."

"Easier said than done, my friend,"

Holt reached into his jacket and was impressed his wallet was still there. He peeled a few dollars and handed them over.

"The Jephfra Hotel, Lev, if you please?"

They drove into the city past cafes and bulletin boards decorated in Hebrew. Tree-lined boulevards thronged with brightly coloured clothes, grim Hasidic black and vivid children's strollers. Silver and yellow buses snaked their way past camels, motor cycles and cars. Rusev didn't seem comfortable looking ahead, turning to make eye-contact seemed more important,

"In Bulgaria, you know how we dealt with narcotics?"

"No?" replied Holt.

A blaring horn and shouts made Rusev glance over the steering wheel.

"We rounded up the drug dealers and 'Poof',"

Rusev's hands left the wheel as he mimed firing a gun with both hands,

"Poof-poof-poof! No more drug dealers. Government take over and sell drugs,"

"That's fascinating, Lev," said Holt, "If you could just…"

He flinched as a truck overtook them then slammed on the brakes. With a stream of Yiddish and Bulgarian obscenities, Rusev hurled his little FIAT around the vehicle.

"Are there drugs here?" asked Holt.

This led to a wide grin,

"Hashish, cocaine, opium - give me an hour, my friend and I can get you anything; women, men, girls, boys – anything is possible here; it's all cha-cha-cha!"

"Just a whiskey and bath will do, Lev," replied Holt.

The FIAT's open windows offered little respite from the humidity and heat.

Everywhere there were hoardings up and billboards in vibrant hues, depicting a solitary chess piece; a queen.

"Something special happening?" asked Holt

"A chess tournament," said Rusev, "Our own Arie Rosenberg up against Blumenfeld, Reshevsky and Szabo. Big news here."

Chess tournament, thought Holt.

"Which player would be the American,"

Rusev hand's left the wheel and waved wildly,

"Blumenfeld!" he roared.

The FIAT slewed and pitched. Holt thought his gelato was on its way back up.

They skidded to a halt outside of the Jephfra Hotel.

"The Café Californian at eight?" said Holt.

"Until then, my friend," said Rusev, "keep the sunglasses,"

Holt watched the FIAT career into the afternoon traffic.

He checked in and handing the concierge a couple of dollars requested he book a ticket for the following day's chess tournament.

"Come to think of it, make it two tickets; I'm a fan of the American," said Holt.

His room was on the third floor. It had narrow open windows and a small balcony. The bed was a solid brass-looking affair and the sea breeze made everything cool. He locked the door, slung the battered case onto the bed and he stripped.

Padding naked into the bathroom he ran the shower.

He shaved and lay on the bed. He fell into a sudden and deep sleep.

He slept for two hours.

SIXTEEN

Tel Aviv

When Holt awoke he glanced at the little square clock; it was 3pm. He filled a glass from a pitcher of water on the dresser. He gulped it down. From the suitcase he pulled out loose slacks, a poorly ironed shirt and fresh socks. He lit a cigarette from the hotel matchbook and immediately thought of Marianne Aubuchon. He checked his watch then realised in the fog of waking up, he no longer possessed one. His wrists were still badly marked from the braids in Lanzmann's chateau. From the bottom of the suitcase, sewn into the inside lining was the ruby removed from Marianne's arm. He put on the sunglasses and took the stairs down to reception. The concierge drew on a small pad the location of The Andaman Ruby Corporation.

Holt thanked him and handed over his door key. A small fold of US dollars followed, met by a wide smile.

The afternoon heat and steel driven pulse of the city made his mind up for him. He'd walk. After half an hour, he arrived at the junction of Geula Street and sat under the cool awning of a cafe. He ordered a double espresso and biscotti. The Andaman Ruby Corporation, for all its grandeur, seemed to be a single window above a shop across the road accessed by a side door. He asked the waiter who shrugged his shoulders; he had never heard of such a business. Holt finished, left a tip and crossed the street.

He pushed the doorbell with the badly typed name above it. It clicked open and Holt ascended the damp smelling staircase. On the first floor he came to a frosted glass door with faded gold ink reading **'A.R.Co.'**. He tried the handle and it opened on hinges in dire need of oil. Inside was a solitary office desk, a few telephones stacked unused at one end. The blinds on the window were half closed and hanging lower on one side. A janitor was at the end of the room with his back to him, sweeping the floor.

"Hello?" said Holt.

The janitor turned. Perhaps it was the speed that alerted Holt. The determined face was one of his torturers, the Lenin look-alike. His hand seemed to snag in his loose-fitting overalls. Holt grabbed one of the telephones on the pile and threw it at him. It glanced off the man, halted in its flight by the trailing extension cord. The stack of phones clattered to the ground in a cacophony of bells. Whatever the man was wrestling with came out of the pocket. It looked like a small square-shaped gun. Holt leaped back through the doorway dragging the door behind him. The glass became a lattice-work of cracks as a bullet hole appeared in the middle of it.

Ostrovsky muttered under his breath. He had two cartridges remaining both with dum-dum heads. Lanzmann had dispatched him and Kvashnin to Tel Aviv to track down Burnett. Lanzmann assumed Burnett would go to these offices. Ostrovsky hadn't expected the recently deceased Richard Ives to walk through the door. Ostrovsky yanked it open. The glass shattered onto the floor. He aimed the little gun and it popped once. Holt lurched forward, stumbling over himself and felt the bullet pass him. The wall bloomed old plaster around his shoulders. He came to a halt at the front door. His grip slipped on the metal latch. He turned around. Ostrovsky stopped and steadied himself midway down the narrow stairs and pointed the little gun directly at Holt.

He had no choice. Holt dashed up the stairs two at a time. He was younger and a fraction faster. He gripped an overall's sleeve. He could smell the garlic on Ostrovksy's breath. The shot went wide, the sound nothing more than a whisper. Holt put everything behind his punch. It struck his opponent's throat. Ostrovsky's hands flew up and Holt went low. He delivered a hefty dig into the mid-drift, doubling Ostrovsky over. The narrow stairwell echoed with their grunts and punches. Holt used his forward momentum to drive Ostrovsky up the stairs. Their shoes sought purchase in their struggle. Near the top stair, Holt dragged Ostrovsky slowly around, using the wall as a brace. He absorbed the desperate slaps and punches to his face and forehead. A kick to the shin ran through Holt like an electric shock. He heaved and released Ostrovsky. Ostrovsky was momentarily airborne, his hands flailing at the air. He arched backwards and clattered down the stairs. He hit the last tread on his shoulders and tumbled into the front door, his hips propelling his legs over his head. Ostrovsky lay twisted and dead.

His neck was broken.

Holt limped down the stairs. He came to Ostrovsky and felt for a pulse. It was fading. He dragged Ostrovsky clear of the doorway and sat him up on a stair tread, leaning his head against the wall. Holt produced the ruby and placed it under Ostrovsky's swelling tongue. Lanzmann would get the message soon enough. Holt opened the door and crossed the street, dusting himself down as he went. The tables outside the café were deserted.

At a table inside the café a man reading a newspaper lowered the edge of it and watched Holt walk past the window. The man threw a few coins into the saucer of his cup. He folded the paper up and followed Holt down an alley way and into the market at Neve Tzedek. He watched Holt weave through the crowd and hail a passing taxi. The man waved down another one just behind it.

"There's a hundred in it for you if you follow that cab and stay two cars back," he said.

The driver wanted to be paid up front and was well worth the advance. Halfway along King Georges Street, Holt's taxi pulled in and the man instructed the driver to keep going, but slowly. He watched Holt pay the driver and enter a travel agency. In the window, images of distant lands beckoned. The man took note of the signage over the agency in English and Hebrew: it was called Regal Holidays.

"Keep driving," said the man.

The taxi merged with evening rush hour traffic and disappeared into the maw of the city.

SEVENTEEN

Tel Aviv

The Café Californian glowed in red and green neon. A jukebox blasted out a rock 'n roll song. Young men and women forced a space between the tables and danced. Holt sipped a cold beer and ordered flat breads, spiced cracked olives, hummus and a fish platter. He lit a cigarette. He had once been told that taking a life diminishes a person slightly and the more you did it, the less a human being you became. He contemplated this as Rusev gave a wave followed by a furtive glance around the room.

"Your handiwork hasn't gone unnoticed, my friend," he said,

"It was self-defence. He had a gun," said Holt.

"The ruby?"

"A message. There's another agent, his side-kick. A woman."

"You're like a bulyzhnik in a pond, Holt. The ripples keep appearing out of nowhere. I'll let my superiors know about this other agent."

"She might be here in Tel Aviv, she's extremely dangerous. She hurt a friend," said Holt.

"Ah, a friend – pretty, I bet?" said Rusev.

"Very."

Rusev grinned at the young waitress, his back teeth amid the stubble glinted like a Clondike gold strike. He ordered vine leaves and salad,

"Watching your figure, Lev?" said Holt.

"I have other business in the city this evening,"

"About that; I'm being followed,"

"Followed?"

"A cab followed me. One of yours? Mossad?" said Holt.

"No."

"Can you find out then?"

"Tel Aviv is a snake pit, my friend," said Rusev, "They could be muggers, assassins or just curious about a very handsome young Englishman."

He raised his hands outward to Holt's cold stare,

"I'll ask, Holt. Now can we enjoy?"

"It's on me, Lev,"

"Even better, Holt."

The vine leaves appeared. Rusev popped them into his mouth whole. He wiped the viscous oil with the back of his hand.

"I need you to reach out to them; your contacts. Allow me safe passage down Highway 20 to Lydda," said Holt.

"All I can do is ask. Ask-ask-ask! - now, Holt, let us sit back and enjoy the pretty waitresses – look around you – food, dancing, girls, yes?"

Holt ordered another beer. Dorothy Jones from Cambridge hadn't been working at the front desk of Regal Holidays that afternoon. Her manager, a tall dapper Englishman unsuitably attired for the heat had met him instead. Holt repeated the codeword on the strip of paper that was just ash in Lydda. Once the manager had confirmed it was correct, Holt had requested a wire transfer of funds and dispatched a coded message to Petrie. The funds had been released and sat fat in his wallet.

"One more thing, Rusev – how much for your car?"

Rusev glanced back, a huge black eyebrow raised,

"It's a heap of shit?"

"How much?"

"Not for sale, my friend"

"Four thousand dollars, Lev. US Dollars. That's probably four times its value. This one-time offer comes without any questions and guaranteed safe passage?"

Lev Rusev contemplated this over his vine leaves. He ate slowly, his eyes staring at Holt. Taking a fork, he reached across and picked at the fish platter.

"You have a deal, my friend."

He spat in his hand and held it out. Holt spat into his and they shook.

"Bring it by the hotel tomorrow evening – and Lev?"

"Yes, Holt?"

"Full of petrol?"

He handed a roll of bills over,

"Two thousand now, two thousand tomorrow."

"Four thousand now. I don't rate your chances."

"Three thousand then," said Holt.

"Deal."

Holt rolled out another thousand.

Rusev's gold flecked grin shone in the electric light. The booths were filled with chatting happy youths. All white T-shirts and slicked back hair. The girls bobbed and weaved to the booming beat of Jerry Lee Lewis from the jukebox and the breath of a sea breeze weaving through the city wafted through the café.

Holt watched Rusev watching the girls and drumming his hands on the table. Jerry Lee Lewis had a point, thought Holt.

There was a whole lotta shakin' going on.

EIGHTEEN

The Accadia Hotel overlooked a small park along the Rothschild Boulevard. Its asymmetrical balconies cast linear shadows across the fresh white concrete. Holt sat on a bench in the park reading a newspaper. From time to time he'd look up at the lines of people queuing to see the chess tournament. The early morning heat and humidity clung about the city. The venue's doors opened, and a crush of bodies pressed into the hotel. Holt waited for the initial surge to pass then folded his paper under his left arm. His shirt was outsized on him, his body grateful for air it captured to flow around him. He adjusted Rusev's sunglasses and produced a crumpled pack of cigarettes. He lit one and looked around the park. Palm trees created a sort of oasis along the freshly tarmacadamed walkways. Bright lines of benches fanned out in geometric rows. Nursing mothers and old women sat with prams and strollers. Holt crushed his cigarette and walked across the road, dodging the dense line of buses.

In the foyer he presented his ticket to an usher and was guided to the main auditorium. His seat was midway and the one beside him was vacant. Overhead fans pulsed, recirculating warm air and body heat. A raised dais with a table with two stop clocks, a chessboard and two comfortable chairs facing each other. A tall chair stood sentinel facing the auditorium; Holt assumed for the umpire. Two name cards in Hebrew were pinned to the side facing the crowd. It was flanked by an enormous chess-board mounted to the wall. On either side of the wall board stood two men in short-sleeved shirts with long poles. A hook hung from each of the mounted boards squares and a stock of black and white cut-outs of rooks, queens and pawns were stacked beside each pole-carrier. As the game progressed the pole carriers would move the pieces across the board for the seats at the back of the auditorium. On either side of each pole carrier hung the American and Israeli flags.

There is a moment before any contest, when the expectation takes an unspoken form, the crowd scenting the competition to come generates a collective mass of electricity. Holt despite his weariness and aches found himself caught up in it. He felt re-energised amid the humanity. An MC came out to applause. He spoke in English and Hebrew. The crowd applauded raucously and rose to its feet when the two chess masters entered from either side. Israel's Rosenberg against America's Blumenfeld. They bowed, shook hands and an umpire took his seat between them. He theatrically wiped his brow with a white handkerchief. The crowd slowly took their seats. Shouts in Russian, German, Yiddish and hearty cheers were met with shushing and *'shut the fuck up*'s. The chess masters bent into their contest.

The vacant seat beside Holt was now occupied,

"Who can find a virtuous woman? For her price is far above rubies," said the man beside him.

"Proverbs 31:10," replied Holt, "King James version."

"Your codename's Chaiwallah, I believe?" said the man. The last part sounded *'arrr'* in its mid-west cadences.

"Cochise," said Holt.

He turned to look at Bill Burnett. The man was quite short. A creased expression with cropped hair and a deep tan smiled, "Nice to meet a friendly face."

"We haven't much time," said Holt.

"How did you know I'd come?"

"You've been following me. It was either here or the Casino."

"The Casino would have been better," said Burnett.

"Here we can talk," said Holt, "I'm told this could go on into the night,"

The first pole carrier slotted Rosenberg's opening gambit, heralded by the MC. The roar from the crowd reverberated around the strobe-lit auditorium.

"Let's watch the game awhile, Chaiwallah. There's always time in this game to take a breather," said Burnett.

"We leave at six. There's an aircraft waiting at Lydda. Its leaving at midnight," said Holt.

Burnett let a shrill whistle as Blumenfeld's white pawn was hooked into battle,

"You're an educated man, right? Familiar with the classics?" said Burnett.

Holt nodded.

"Thucydides?"

"Peloponnesian wars, yes," said Holt.

"An established state, afraid of a new one rising sets out to start a war?"

"France?" said Holt

"Against Uncle Sam. Lanzmann. The Czechs and the Russian's are using him to start a coup d'etat. They're calling it *'Operation Rubis'.*"

First blood had gone to Rosenberg. The crowd were ecstatic. Men and women either side of Holt and Burnett rose to their feet, punched arms, hugged, danced and whistled. The umpire raised his arms for calm. Blumenfeld gathered his face into his hands as he stared at the opponent's positions.

"Give a man like Julius Lanzmann access to a nuclear bomb and one of the largest land armies in Europe? It's the USSR all the way to the English Channel with Germany pincered in. Then North Africa." said Burnett.

"My job is to get you to Lydda and back into France," said Holt.

"That could be tricky. Long way to go for an escort?"

"I have my reasons."

"I hope she was worth it,"

"I hope so too. We just do our best don't we, Cochise?"

"That we do, Chaiwallah."

Holt handed Burnett his hotel key,

"The Jephfra, room 302. The concierge is discreet. Have you cash?"

"Yes,"

"A twenty buys his silence. In the wardrobe is a suitcase. There's a suit in it – beige. Unlikely it will fit. Inside pocket - a passport and driver's licence. Your name is Marc Claes. Wait for me there."

Burnett waited for the next round of wild jubilation and drifted into the crowd. Holt glanced up at the clock perched above the mounted chess board. It was 2pm. He had a few more hours to go.

NINETEEN

No one ever notices the cleaner. Natalia Kvashnin squeezed herself into the maid's uniform in the backroom of the Jephfra Hotel. As she adjusted the lines of her unimaginative beige clothing she placed a syringe full of the Aminazin toxin into the folds of her apron. It was intended for the American. The ornate Cossack knife strapped to her ankle was for the American's escort. Finding Ostrovsky sitting on the stairs of the Andaman Ruby Corporation she had touched his cold expressionless face tenderly, kissing the dead mouth. Then found the ruby with her tongue. Kvashnin was incapable of any real depth of emotion but she still felt some sense of loss. In the wrecked office, she found a working phone. KGB Director Sukachen had been informed. She was told to remain at the office waiting further instruction. She dragged Ostrovsky's body up into the office, stretched out his limp body. She rolled up one of her sleeves and taking the knife, carved a tear-drop into her flesh. When the opportunity would arise, she would take one of her pins and roll a strand of thread around its tip. With a bottle of Indian ink, she would dip the needle and etch the tear permanently into her arm. She lay down and slept beside him. The phone rang. From thousands of miles away in Moscow, Kvashnin was given an address. The Jephfra Hotel – Room 302.

She had slipped in through the hotel service entrance. The kitchens were bustling with lunchtime orders. Spying the lines of cleaning carts, she homed in on a maid. A rabbit punch to the base of the skull had killed the woman instantly. She had dragged the body to a storage cupboard and tossed it in. It didn't matter if it was discovered, Kvashnin would be quick.

She rode the elevator up to the third floor.

*

Holt and Burnett preened and groomed themselves as best they could. The clothes didn't quite fit, but also didn't make them look out of place either. Holt looked around the room one more time. According to the small bedside clock it was almost 6pm. Holt stowed the empty suitcase under the bed. He had no need for it now. They had two new identities from the Parisian veteran's hospital and Holt hoped Rusev would keep his end of the bargain. Burnett knotted a garish kipper tie.

There was a knock at the door.

"Room service," said a woman's voice.

Holt opened the door. It exploded in on its hinges.

He took an open-handed punch to the face at full force knocking him onto the floor. The maid came in through the doorway like a dervish. She delivered a karate blow to the side of Burnett's head that stunned him and sent him wheeling onto the bed. Holt staggered to his feet. He recognised the woman. The amber eyes were narrowed to a slit and her hair had come undone. Her teeth were bared, her face contorted. A glint of metal flashed across Holt's vision. His nose felt swollen and wet. He gripped her arm. Blood was running down his face. He could taste it. She could smell it – it sent a surge of power through her. She head-butted him. Holt saw a myriad of exploding stars.

"Burnett," he shouted.

Kavashnin and Holt grappled knocking over chairs, cabinets and lamps.

Burnett began to stir.

Holt had to use both hands to hold Kvashnin's arm. She spread her legs for greater purchase and worked her free arm around Holt's neck. He could feel his air supply being cut off. The blade began to turn towards his face. Burnett finally sprang into action. He lurched off the bed tackling both. The trio crashed onto the floor. Kvashnin elbowed Burnett into the face and rolled free of them. She leapt up and took a few steps back. In one hand was her knife, the other a syringe. She crouched ready to attack.

Holt grabbed an overturned lamp and threw it. It missed but wrong footed her. Holt and Burnett dashed to her and Burnett's hand was slashed. He hissed in pain and grabbed her arm. Holt punched her hard above her eyebrows. The amber light dimmed for a fraction. It was long enough for Holt to release the syringe from her grip and jab it in her neck.

A momentary flash of horror swept across her face then the eyelids fluttered shut. She collapsed onto the floor. They stretched her out onto the bed. Once they had straightened the room as best they could, they grabbed bathroom towels to stem the flow of their blood. Holt was afraid to look in the mirror.

He went to the balcony. It was too far up to jump.

"Service elevator," he said.

"Well, what are we waiting for?" said Burnett.

Outside the hotel, Rusev's FIAT sat parked on the kerb. Holt and Burnett dashed to it avoiding startled glances. The keys were in. Holt started it. The petrol tank was full.

"Next stop Paris," he said.

"Here's hoping," said Burnett.

He opened the glove compartment.

"No gun?" he said.

"You were hoping for one?" said Holt.

Holt nudged the car out onto the street and then accelerated to the junction that would lead them out onto H-20.

"They come in kinda handy sometimes," said Burnett.

Holt had to agree.

TWENTY

Ely, Cambridge.

Petrie and Broughton-Ware kept glancing at the antique brass clock on the marble mantlepiece. The comfortable chairs placed at angles to the aged hearth blocked the warm breeze coming in from the garden. Standing at the open French doors that overlooked the dried-out grass and neglected blooms stood Laidlaw. He smoked a cigarette. He stared up at the fish scale clouds hanging in the sky. Turning on his hip he stared at the clock too. Petrie rose from his chair to stretch his muscles and walked toward Laidlaw. His attention was caught by a hulking rusted lawn roller abandoned near a rockery.

"Holt?" asked Laidlaw.

"En-route I believe," replied Petrie.

"Very good. Very good – 'Cochise'?"

"With him. Holt was very vague on the details – only that he'd be arriving today."

"Was there much disruption?"

"A little, but things are now under control."

"Excellent. Dewar will inform the Americans. The Foreign Office will take it from here, Petrie."

Broughton-Ware unfolded himself from his chair, placing a battered leather tome on the floor. The staid atmosphere marked by the tick of the clock on the mantlepiece dispersed at the sound of a car. The three men stood in the hallway. A Jaguar XK150 drove up the winding driveway, its engine growling on low revs. Broughton-Ware walked out to meet it. A rare smile appeared.

"I have it on good authority that General de Gaulle will take over France," said Laidlaw, "wheels are in motion and all that,"

"Julius Lanzmann?"

"Found hanged in the kitchen of his chateau – suicide apparently. Authorities are investigating."

"Unfortunate."

"Indeed. The Russian's would never hesitate in burning a deep asset to avoid an unnecessary conflict with the west."

"What about Burma?"

"Lanzmann's offices at The Andaman Ruby Corporation in Hanthawaddy suffered a set-back. Industrial explosion in the ruby mine. No casualties."

"What a relief."

"I was stationed there in '48. Beautiful country, no self-respecting Englishwoman would travel there though; not with India just over the border. I policed these colonial stations, six thousand feet up – cool air, no malaria, no cholera. Churches, cottages and clubs – little pockets of England high up in the clouds."

Petrie watched Holt get out. Holt had an enormous white plaster stretched across his nose. The sunglasses straddling it looked like they had seen better days. A smaller tanned more pugilistic man got out of the passenger side. Bill Burnett stood and shook Broughton-Ware's hand. He placed his arm around Holt's shoulder and gave it a good-natured punch.

"Was he a Russian asset?" asked Petrie,

"Just another disenchanted American. He's the CIA's problem now," said Laidlaw.

Petrie tamped fresh tobacco into a pipe and lit it. He offered the lighter to Laidlaw who lit up a Dunhill,

"The Burmese have a saying, *'The bigger the tiger, the larger the footprint'*, and I think we're going to be dealing with bigger tigers these days," said Laidlaw.

They walked to the doorway and welcomed *'Cochise'* in.

TWENTY-ONE

Paris

The Sainte-Anne Hospital gallery looked over a small courtyard. The bunting hanging from the arches of red, white and blue wafted in the summer breeze. In the small well-tended garden, clutches of lavender seduced the bees. Unlike the veteran's hospital, Sainte-Anne's silence felt enforced, thought Holt. At the end of the gallery, slumped in a wheel-chair sat Marianne Aubuchon. For a second, Holt thought he saw a very old woman. A few strands of hair fluttered about her head. He felt guilty about his recuperation. He resented his healing. The crunch of shoes made him look over his shoulder. The young and earnest Dr. Fournel held out a hand.

"I received your telegram, Monsieur, if you have a moment?"

"No, I don't," said Holt.

He walked over to a patch of Lavender. Selecting a few bunches, he pulled them up and bound the sheaf with a long strand of grass. He squatted down in front of Marianne and placed the lavender in her hands. He thought he could see the veins through the skin, as if she were some sort of double-exposure, fading in the light.

"For you, Aubuchon," he said.

She didn't recognise him. She stared ahead.

She clutched the lavender. Holt touched her hand.

Fournel hooked his thumbs into his tweed waistcoat beneath his white coat. An old-fashioned pocket watch chain caught the sunlight. His hair was carefully pomaded and parted. His beard was unkempt.

"Unresponsive?" said Holt.

"Electroconvulsive therapy was unsuccessful," said Fournel.

"You electrocuted her?"

"It's an acceptable treatment,"

"No. No it is not, who decided this?"

"Not I, Monsieur Holt. She was transferred here. We know what she was injected with. It has resulted in a severe form of catatonia, possible schizophrenia and extreme shock. We are trying various therapies."

"Her mother lives in Marseilles,"

"Mademoiselle Aubuchon has no living next of kin,"

The day was getting warmer, Holt eased the wheelchair into the cooling shade of the stone.

"Reserpine, Dopamine, Chlorpromazine?" asked Holt.

"All very experimental, Monsieur Holt and very, very expensive?"

"I can afford it."

"We know, but we have no idea of the side-effects?"

"Anything is better than this," said Holt.

"I'm not going to kill a patient on a whim, on a *crime passionnel*, Monsieur? We are doing everything we can. It will take time."

Holt stared out at the garden. The hospital's walls muffled the sound of the city creating an oasis of silence.

"May I have a chair. Have you paper, pencil?" said Holt.

Fournel retuned with a fold-up chair. He handed Holt an old wooden clipboard with a few sheets of blank paper.

"I've other patients to attend to – adieu, Monsiuer."

Holt pulled up alongside Aubuchon,

"Good afternoon, Marianne, my name is Sebastian. Shall we do a little drawing?"

Holt drew a squat uneven-looking heart. He drew a line coming out of the top. He then drew two tear-shaped lines on either side of the line,

"Now, Marianne, this is an apple – 'A' is for Apple,"

Marianne and Holt sat for the afternoon in the shade of the stone gallery writing out the alphabet to the music of the bees.

THE END

The Road of a Thousand Tigers ©2018

*

My Thanks for answering emails and endless enquiries,

Vanessa Fox O'Loughlin – @ Inkwell Group / Writing.ie.

Howard Jackson – @ Red Rattle Books.

Ellis Shuman – author (ellisshuman.blogspot.com)

Nisea Doddy Burke – @ The Shelbourne Hotel, Dublin.

Author Bio:

Robert Craven was born in Manchester and now lives in Dublin, Ireland. He is the author of:

Get Lenin.

Zinnman.

A Finger of Night.

Hollow Point.

The Steampunk Novella – The Mandarin Cipher.

He is also featured in two horror anthologies:

'A communion of blood' a Vampire short published in 'Broken Mirrors Fractured minds' – Vamptasy Press.

'Vodou' in Red Rattle Book's 'Zombie Bites'.

Twitter @cravenrobert

The Road of a Thousand Tigers

Printed in Great Britain
by Amazon